Tales of Damnation

by

I0536704

William Blackwell

Tales of Damnation

Published by William Blackwell Publishing
Paperback ISBN: 978-1-0697318-9-0
Version: 2021.03.15

Do not go gentle into that good night,
Old age should burn and rave at close of day;
Rage, rage against the dying of the light.
—Dylan Thomas

Beware that, when fighting monsters, you yourself do
not become a monster... For when you gaze long into
the abyss, the abyss gazes also into you.

—Frederich W. Nietzsche

Of such great powers or beings there may be conceivably a
survival... a survival of a hugely remote period when...
consciousness was manifested perhaps, in shapes and forms long
since withdrawn before the tide of advancing humanity... forms
of which poetry and legend alone have caught a flying memory
and called them gods, monsters, mythical beings of all sorts and
kinds...

—Algernon Blackwood

Table of Contents

The Spot

Balboa, or that's what he liked to be called anyway, moseyed through the raucous house party. A stop here. A pretty blonde. A wink. A flexing of his six-pack abs, clearly visible through the skin-tight muscle shirt. A look from her. *That should equal a little fun in the midnight moon a little later.* He moved smoothly through a gregarious, laughing crowd, heading to the rum punch bowl, but not before another stop, another wink, and this time flexing his right bicep to an attractive brunette. Blonde or brunette, it mattered not to Balboa. He was built like a brick shithouse, and very proud of that fact. It got him attention. It got him respect. It got him laid, which was what was on his mind now. He reached the punch bowl and, using the oversized serving spoon, refilled his plastic cup.

He noticed a scrawny, nerdish-looking dude loitering around the punch bowl blinking furtively at the throngs of revelers, evidently lacking the self-confidence to approach anyone.

"You too shy?" Balboa said, extending a meat hook. "I'm Balboa."

The man's eyes widened at Balboa's imposing, muscle-bound physique. "A little bit." Then he hesitated, spilled a little rum punch onto a pencil-stuffed shirt pocket, and nervously offered his hand. "Ralph."

Balboa squeezed, grinning as he watched the little man's face flush with pain. When he released his iron grip a few seconds later—a few seconds too long—Ralph quickly withdrew his hand, set his drink down, and began rubbing his knuckles.

"That's a vice-grip you have," Ralph said, a single tear sprouting and glistening on his lower left eyelid.

"Oh, that," Balboa said, looking approvingly at his massive forearm and bicep. "My old man always told me that a firm handshake is a sign of self-confidence and strength. Nobody wants a wet rag. Right?"

Ralph wiped his eye, studied his reddening hand, picked up his drink, and gulped two large mouthfuls. "I guess so. You... you look familiar. Is Balboa your real name?"

"No. Brad Powers. But everyone calls me Balboa." He racked his brain trying to remember where he might have met this little twerp before. In the cavernous space between his ears, nothing materialized.

Ralph took a few steps back as two women approached the punch bowl. "You mean as in Rocky Balboa? From the movie, *Rocky*."

"You got it, Einstein," Balboa said, a spark of recognition flashing across brain circuits but shorting out before producing a mental image. As the giggling women approached the punch bowl, Balboa scooped up the ladle and pushed the punch toward the ladies.

"Sure," a pretty blonde said, holding her plastic cup unsteadily above the trickling pink liquid. "Don't mind if I do, and thank you, Mr. Strong Man."

"You're very welcome, my dear."

The other woman, a short-haired bubbly brunette, extended her cup and Balboa seamlessly refilled it.

She grinned drunkenly, attempting but failing to curl her hand around his massive bicep. It was like trying to wrap a paper clip around a sledge hammer. "Wow, you're strong. You're huge."

"I am indeed," he said. "And you're only scratching the surface."

Both women laughed.

Ralph backed up a few steps.

"Who's your friend?" the short-haired brunette said after the laughter had subsided.

"That's Ralph," Balboa said. "He's not my friend. And I'm Balboa."

"Ralph?" the blonde said. "He looks like he's gonna be sick."

All three of them laughed boisterously. Ralph silently shrank to the size of a mouse.

The brunette hugged Balboa's bicep with both arms and brought her mouth close to his ear. "We're over there," she whispered, gesturing with a finger. "I'm Sarah and my friend is Sandra. Come and join us and we'll promise you a little more than scratching the surface."

She kissed him on the cheek and both women wobbled off. Balboa watched as they joined hands in an effort to stabilize one another, weaved out onto the dance floor, spun around, and simultaneously winked at him, seductively licking their pouty red lips.

Balboa polished his drink, refilled it, and turned to Ralph, who had returned to the rum punch table and was now leaning on it like it was the only thing in the world propping him up.

"Excuse me, I have to go rescue two damsels in distress," Balboa said. "Duty calls."

"You have something on your face," Ralph said.

Balboa had always prided himself on his impeccably clear complexion and chiseled warrior-like features. "What?"

"It's a spot. Looks like skin cancer to me."

"Where?" Balboa said, worry lines creasing his youthful face.

Ralph pointed below Balboa's right eye. "Right there. On your cheek. I'd get that checked out if I were you. Melanoma's a bitch. Fast-spreading cancer. Can kill you off in a matter of weeks."

It was likely just an eerie coincidence, but Balboa felt a tingling sensation exactly on the spot that Ralph had pointed to. He flushed and a vein popped on his temple and snaked its way down toward the spot, creating a slight stinging sensation. *Fucking jealous loser.*

From his peripheral vision, Balboa noticed Sarah and Sandra off in the corner of the large home, seductively gyrating their tight little asses on a tabletop and waving to him. He knew it was only a matter of time before some other drunken losers would move in and try to take over where he'd left off. *No fucking way.*

But the fear snaking up his esophagus was palpable. He touched the spot on his cheek, took a few deep breaths, and tried to assure himself that it was only the tiny scar left over from a small cut he'd suffered from a brawl a few weeks ago. He'd flattened an acid-witted loser with a straight right to the jaw in the parking lot outside of a bar after the man had upstaged him in front of an attractive woman he had been oh-so close to closing. Surprisingly, the man had gotten to his feet a few seconds after the shot, smashed a beer bottle in half on the lid of a metal garbage can, and swiped at his face. A sharp edge of the bottle had sliced his cheek before he'd hammered the man with an uppercut and knocked him out cold. After the incident, the malignant narcissist that he was, Balboa had carefully disinfected the wound before applying a topical antibiotic and bandaging it with a small circular adhesive Band-Aid. A week later, he'd grimaced at the small quarter-inch scar in the mirror; yet he'd finally come to terms with it, reassuring himself that "battle scars add character and make you look tough."

Ralph was grinning at him now. "I see you're worried about it. As I said, I'd get it checked out if I were you. Melanoma's a bitch."

But Balboa found his usual arrogant confidence, seeing Ralph steal a longing look at the gyrating hotties. "I'd invite you over as a wing-man. But who the hell wants a shy, chicken-shit wing-man anyway?"

He spun around and walked purposefully toward his prey. A hunter he was. A hunter he would always be.

***

More than Balboa's big head was throbbing the following morning after waking up in a strange and disheveled apartment in Calgary's downtown core. He blinked a couple of times, gouged the sleep from his eyes, and watched as two blanketed heads bobbed and weaved, expertly working his swollen member. He lay back on the pillow, reminisced about the wild threesome last night, and enjoyed the carnal pleasures of the here and now as Sandra and Sarah expertly sucked him to a shuddering climax.

Sarah pulled the blanket away, licked her lips, and wiped a sticky milky ribbon from her chin. She winked. "I see you enjoyed that."

"I did. Thank you."

"You were a fucking stud," Sandra said, popping out from underneath the blanket and rushing into the bathroom.

Sarah wiped her sticky finger on Balboa's leg, stood up, and held out her hand. "I think you got your money's worth. That'll be six hundred bucks. And a bargain at that."

"Call it eight hundred," Sandra said from the bathroom as the pitter-patter of water droplets could be heard cascading into the shower. "Two hundred more for the blowjob."

"Right," Sarah said. "Eight hundred it is then."

Despite the throbbing in his head, Balboa got out of bed quickly and grabbed his underwear. As he put them on, he said, "What? I never agreed to that."

Sarah stepped forward and jabbed her index finger into his muscled chest. "Oh, yes, you did. Now cough up. By the way, what's that spot on your face? Looks like melanoma to me. Melanoma is a killer, you know."

In a lightning-fast move, Balboa reached out and grabbed her hand, twisting it back at an awkward angle as she winced, groaned, and quickly bent to her knees. Subdued. He applied a little more pressure, comfortable in the knowledge it would be smarting for a few minutes and would give him a chance to get dressed and escape. The other bitch was in the shower. Occupied.

As Sarah shouted and screamed, Balboa scrambled around the apartment, picking up his clothes and dressing. In no time, he approached the door, checking his back pocket, feeling for his wallet, exhaling a deep sigh when he felt the warm and leathery, cash-stuffed mound.

Then the dim recollection surfaced. Balboa, in his drunken stupor, had agreed to the threesome. Had agreed to the fee. And he had the money. On him. Thanks to a two-million-dollar inheritance three years ago from his deceased mother—he was still angry that his snobby sister had received ten million—he wasn't hurting for cash. That inheritance had allowed him to quit his security guard job, downsize, invest modestly, and live off the interest. And pursue his dream. Prey on women. Intimidate men. But he wasn't the kind of guy to throw money around, even if he *had* agreed to it.

As he opened the door, he heard a loud *clang* and felt a sharp pain on the back of his head. Dazed, confused, and seeing stars, he spun around to see Sandra, buck naked and dripping wet, grinning and holding a cast-iron frying pan high in the air. She raised it, coming down for another strike. Reflexively, he brought his right pipe up. She slammed the frying pan down hard on it, so hard it squirted loose from her hand and bounced on the front porch of the house as Balboa, blood dripping profusely from the head wound, staggered out the door, found some momentum, and fled.

***

Two weeks later, Balboa waited anxiously in the skin cancer specialist waiting room. He was dazed for at least a day or two after the blunt force head trauma, but he hadn't bothered to get it diagnosed, instead taking it easy until the goose egg had subsided and his head cleared. But he had sought a diagnosis for the spot on his face, the one that fucktard Ralph had pointed out. He had called his doctor and gotten a referral to a dermatologist—one Doctor Ray Burman.

He had become obsessed with the spot, analyzing it ad nauseam every day in the mirror. He had even begun to have terrifying nightmares of the spot growing rapidly, covering his entire body and destroying his cells, and decimating his body one agonizing cell at a time.

The waiting room was full of patients and he had already been waiting for nearly an hour. One woman entered and sat next to him. Her face was mostly covered with a white blood-stained bandage.

She focused with one bulbous eye on the spot. "Looks like melanoma to me. That's what I got. I have to get half my face cut off. Complete facial reconstruction."

Balboa didn't respond, looking away as he felt this morning's bacon and eggs churn in his stomach and start clawing up his throat—an acidic puke ball. He swallowed hard, tasted egg, bacon, horseradish, orange juice, and coughed.

"You might be lucky," the cancer-stricken woman said. "Mine is stage four. There is no stage five you know. Well, I guess there is, but it's six feet under." Her mouth opened, exposing rotten teeth. A single drop of blood leaked out, clinging precariously to her bandage-wrapped chin.

Balboa felt a bead of perspiration pop on his forehead, dribble down his head, and lodge in his bushy eyebrow. He wiped it away, tried unsuccessfully to smile, then got up and sat in another chair. She was starting to creep him out big-time.

She tssk-tssked him away with a pointed finger.

He picked up an outdoor adventure magazine and began flipping through the pages, seeing but not seeing the kayaks, mountains, campfires, lakes, rivers, and wildlife. Would this be his last chance to really live? *Everything's gonna be okay. It's nothing. You're gonna be fine. You're gonna be fine.*

His mind drifted back to where it had all begun. Ralph. His nerdy image had popped into his head a few times lately, and he was still dumbfounded as to how he knew the man. *If I see him again, maybe I should apologize. Fuck that. Fuck him.* Just as a dim recollection of where he knew Ralph from began to settle over him, he heard his name called.

"Brad Powers?"

"That's me."

"Doctor Burman will see you now."

He wiped a sweaty brow and stood. "O... Okay."

Five minutes later, Doctor Burman, holding a large and sophisticated magnifying glass, stepped back, a pained expression on his face.

"What's wrong?" Balboa said. "Am I gonna be okay?"

Doctor Burman put the magnifying glass down and rubbed his knee. "My knee hurts," he said. "The joys of old age. It's arthritis."

Balboa felt little sympathy for the aging white-haired man. "What about the spot?"

Doctor Burman slowly removed rubber gloves and tossed them in a wastebasket. He went to a sink, scrubbed his hands, dried them with paper towels, crumpled them, and tossed them into a wastebasket. "We'll have to cut it out and get it biopsied. That'll tell us for sure what it is. But to my trained eye, and I've been doing this for over thirty years, it's a very common, slow-moving skin cancer. You're gonna be fine. Nothing to worry about. Make an appointment with my receptionist and I'll see you in a week or two."

Out on the busy street, soaking up cancer-giving rays of bright morning sunshine, Balboa was elated. He felt like he had a new lease on life. Maybe it wasn't too late. Not too late to turn his self-serving ways around. Track down Ralph. Apologize. Return to Sarah and Sandra's house. Pay them out, even give them a handsome tip. Say sorry. Write down the names of all the people he'd wronged. Right the wrongs. Make amends.

"That's it," he shouted, jumping for joy, tripping on the cross-walk curb, and falling head-first into the busy intersection. He rolled on the pavement, started to get up, and then his mouth dropped open in horror as he saw the speeding bus descend on him.

Crunch... crunch... crunch!

Balboa felt his bones snapping like brittle twigs as the large tires squashed and splattered him into the pavement. He felt his skull caving and cracking, his eyes popping from his sockets.

The bus dragged him along the road for a city block before the tires spat his crumpled and bloody remains curbside.

As the last vestiges of life drained from Balboa, he *remembered* Sarah, Sandra, and Ralph. He had used and abused the two women in high school, probably devastated their self-esteem and led them into prostitution. One night stands. Dropped them like a ton of bricks. He had bullied Ralph to no end, mercilessly stripping the man of his self-esteem and self-confidence—helping to mold the loser that Ralph had become.

But as the skeletal hand of the grim reaper slowly cloaked him in blackness, he realized three things: *It's too late for redemption. Karma's a bitch. And then you die.*

The Cab Ride

"Where did you say we were going?" Rex Anderson asked, gazing around in confusion at the dark and unfamiliar surroundings.

"I didn't," the cab driver said, scrunching his brow. "You're supposed to tell me."

"Right." Rex stalled. *Where the hell am I? Where am I going?* "What city are we in?"

The cabbie craned his neck and looked in the back seat, slit-eyes narrowing. His bald head was bulbous and sweat-soaked. His face was grizzled with what Rex surmised was a four-day growth, not quite short enough to be fashionable and not long enough to call a beard. Scruff.

"Are you kidding me?" the cabbie said, pulling over. "I just picked you up at the Vancouver International Airport and you're telling me you don't know where the hell you are or where the hell you're going? That must've been some flight."

But try as he might, Rex couldn't remember the flight. He remembered something he'd read about lucid dreaming, waking up in a dream and realizing it was a dream. Maybe that's what this was. The article said to look for signs you're dreaming. Look at your hand. Look away. Look back at it. If it's a five-fingered balloon, you're dreaming. If it's normal, you're not. Rex tried it. His hand appeared normal. *Think. Right, Dad lives in Vancouver. He's sick. Dying.* "I think I want to see my dad."

"Okay," the cabbie said. "We're making some progress. Where does your father live?"

"Almdale Crescent. Up by the university. Number 36 Almdale Crescent."

As the cabbie pulled out into bustling evening traffic, Rex took stock of his surroundings, hoping that he wasn't losing his mind. The landscape looked eerily surreal. Black and pink sky. No moon. No stars. Red and white headlight and taillight beams dancing all around, periodically leaping high into the night sky. Absent was the steady hissing of the traffic.

He tried to assemble the pieces of this twisted jigsaw puzzle. He wasn't one to lose his mind, nor his memory for that matter. He hardly ever dreamed, or at least if he did, he remembered very little the morning after. He had a stable life in Ontario. Good job as an accountant in a prestigious accounting firm. Only 33, and moving up the ladder fast. He'd recently started dating a hot redhead, whom he believed was the love of his life. Everything had been going just peachy.

But then the calls had started coming. First from his mom, who'd long ago divorced his father even though they'd remained friends; then his sister; then his other sister; and finally some of his close Vancouver friends, telling him to come home and help to get his father in a nursing home. At 89, Seth Anderson had broken his hip last year. That accident, and ever-present arthritis in both of his knees, had landed him in a walker, barely able to move around the house, scarcely able to get into a commode, and unable to care for himself. But he had stubbornly refused to go to a nursing home, as much as everyone had tried to convince him otherwise. And the family felt Rex was the only person who could convince him that now was that time. Rex was the favorite son, the star of the show, the one in high school who'd been voted most likely to succeed. The one who *had* succeeded. They called him the family patriarch, but he wanted nothing to do with that title and, as much as he hated to admit it, wanted little to do with his father right now, even though he had been spoiled as a child, had been his father's favorite child, and had been loved to death during his critical child-rearing years.

Rex sighed. *Am I like so many other kids? Forgetting about their mothers and fathers in their time of need. Abandoning them when it mattered the most. No. I'm going to fix this.*

"We're almost there," the cabbie said. "Another five minutes."

The comment unleashed a flood of memories. Samantha and Cindy, his two sisters who had stepped up to the plate and begun caring for Seth regularly, even though both of them were struggling financially and juggling a house full of rug-rats of their own, had apprised Rex of the condition of the home. Bed bugs. Mold. Unfixed stray and spraying cats. And at best the house had deteriorated into a fixer-upper. At worst, a knockdown that health inspectors, if they knew, would quickly declare it unfit for human habitation and condemn it. *A health hazard. A death trap. It's a fucking death trap.*

"I don't want to go there," Rex said, a bead of perspiration popping on his forehead and rolling into his eye. He wiped it with a hand, the stinging salt blurring his vision incomprehensibly in both eyes. Rex felt around the dimly lit back seat for his knapsack. Nothing. His cell phone. No dice.

The cabbie slowed, craned his neck, and stared at Rex, veins popping in his forehead and neck. Popping, pulsating, pounding. His slit-eyes were fiery red and a forked serpent's tongue slithered from his mouth as he spoke: "You go to your house and care for your ailing father. Look at all he's done for you."

How does he know? But there was no time for that. "No. There must be hotels around here. Take me to a hotel. Any hotel."

"There are no hotels around here," the cabbie said. "Just your father's house."

"Look, I'll help him," Rex said, panic rising in his voice. "I... I just can't stay there. It's... it's unsafe."

The taxi screeched to a stop and the rear passenger door automatically opened. "Get the fuck out," the cabbie said. "Now!"

"Please, take me to a hotel. I'll help him. I just can't stay there."

A long-barreled handgun appeared in the cabbie's hand and he stuffed the barrel between Rex's eyes.

Rex heard a horrifying click.

"Now!!"

Rex reached into his jeans pocket, produced a hundred dollar bill, and tossed it on the back seat. The door closed swiftly, automatically, and the taxi sped away, spitting dirt, gravel, and tufts of grass into Rex's face.

Rex shielded his face and screamed, a long, drawn-out, blood-curdling affair. He bolted upright in bed. "No, no, no," he said, darting into the hallway, stopping suddenly, and realizing with a long sigh that indeed he had been dreaming. He was drenched in sweat, his heart was pounding in his chest, and his hands were trembling. As he stumbled toward the bathroom to splash some cold water onto his face, the phone rang.

He picked it up and answered without looking at the call display.

"Rex?" his sister Samantha said.

"Yeah. It's me."

"You had your chance. And you blew it. Dad's dead."

Fire and Fury

I don't know why I felt so much trepidation about venturing into the forest. Normally Mother Nature brings me great joy. Yesterday, I even learned a new word—werifesteria—the human desire to wander through the woods aimlessly in search of magic and mystery. So where was my werifesteria this evening? Sipping a coffee on the back porch of my humble abode on 60 acres of Prince Edward Island paradise—with 2000 feet of pristine oceanfront—I tried to put a finger on the reason for my frayed nerves and jangled senses.

I looked to the sparkling stars and the looming full moon for answers. Nothing. I listened to the hissing of the trees, driven by a 20 mile-per-hour west wind. Still nothing. I looked into the darkness of thick woods, just beyond my manicured lawn. I thought I heard a twig snap. I jumped, spilling hot coffee on my shirt and down my pants.

"What's wrong with you?" I said, snatching a recycled old t-shirt off the balcony railing and wiping myself somewhat dry. I took a couple of deep breaths and sat down. Waited for relative quiet. *What are you waiting for? It's always quiet. Only wind-blown trees hissing. Not even a bird chirping. No twigs snapping. You're hearing things. Think, think, think. Why fear? Why now?*

Even though it was a cool summer evening, I suddenly felt hot. A bead of sweat exploded on my forehead. Dribbled into my eye. The saltiness stung and I wiped it with my hand. *Hot, hot, hot... that's it.*

It came to me in a flash. I have nightmares every night. I remember them at the time, but most of them disappear soon after I wake up. Most of them, I don't write down. Only the really gory ones. This one, I had last night. I didn't write it down, but I still remember it. Remember it like it happened yesterday. Remember it like it's happening right now. In the nightmare, which felt more like a living hell, I woke up in the middle of the night, went outside, climbed into my trusty pickup and drove down a twisted and bumpy road to my waterfront site, about seventy feet from the water's edge. The night before, I had had a rather large bonfire, along with some friends and a few beers, and I wanted to make sure the blaze was extinguished since I had left the site with the fire still burning quite brightly. Flashlight in hand, I arrived at the smoldering ashes, poked them around a bit, and then let out a deep sigh. It wasn't out but pretty damn close. Then I heard a whoosh, felt a hot flash singe my eyebrows, and looked up at a large pine tree. About six feet up its three-foot diameter trunk, it branched out into three trees. In the middle of those three trees, a large bonfire blazed wildly out of control.

With a sinking feeling of despair and helplessness, I scrambled over to the tree, watching in disbelief as the fire's orange tentacles ravaged the three amigos. I knew with a dread certainty that there was nothing I could do. It would burn out of control, burn down my forest, probably ravage me and kill all of my neighbors in that small corner of the island where I live. Then I woke up, heart pounding in my chest, sweat streaming down my face, and screamed at the top of my lungs, "No, no, no... please, God no." And it was the sound of my own voice that had snapped me into reality, assuring me that everything was fine, the forest wasn't burning, I wasn't gonna burn, and my neighbors on the island weren't gonna die. The fire was out.

Or was it? I wondered. *Hell hath no fury like Mother Nature scorned.*

I have a confession to make. I'm a pyromaniac. Even as a kid, I loved starting fires. I'm not talking arson kind of fires. Just the ones you have when you're camping, or the ones you sneak out and light in your backyard when your parents are asleep. Everything about fires has always fascinated me. The glow. The heat. The dancing flames. The magic. The mystery. Even fireworks. Sparklers. Shooting stars. Rockets. Firecrackers. As kids, we used to have firecracker fights, lobbing them idiotically at each other's heads, and if we got really lucky, shoving them down some unsuspecting fool's pants and watching them shriek in agony as their asses exploded. Lol. Hilarious, right?

But, as an adult, I developed a healthy respect for fire. My mother used to tell me, "You play with fire, son, and you will get burned. It's not a question of if, it's when."

And of course, Mom was right. Clearing an old logging road and a beachfront site, my disrespect and underestimation of Mother Nature came back to scorch me in the ass. Burns to my hair. My eyebrows. My arms. My legs. More than once my clothes caught on fire. Most of my fireside clothes are pock-marked with burn holes. Fortunately, none of those burns were life-threatening. My ass didn't explode, thank God. And, believe it or not, the burns to my clothes and flesh were not what terrified me the most.

During the beachfront clearing operation, I hired a logger to help me with the project. I decided to burn some of the logging slash as we worked, telling him I had a safe, albeit makeshift fire pit. His name was Norman but I called him Normandy. He was as big as the country. Watching me pile twigs in an open area, he eyed me with skepticism, concern, and a healthy dose of fear. "Be careful with that, Gary. It's a hot and dry day. Don't make it too big."

I looked at him, oozing arrogance and over-confidence. "Don't worry, Normandy. I've got this."

Like hell I did.

As soon as I lit the pile of twigs, it went up in a flash. Seconds later, flames shot through the dry moss forest floor like mission-bound streaks of lightning—bee-lining it straight for the nearby trees and stumps. It was like an octopus's poison tentacles, fanning out in all directions.

Seized by unbridled panic, I started dashing around, stomping out the hot tentacles of fire. Normandy immediately dropped his chainsaw, picked up a nearby shovel, and began frantically pounding out the flames. Fortunately, after about a minute—that seemed like an hour—we had most of it contained. We met at a tree-stump that had ignited, me foot-stomping, Normandy pounding with the shovel until finally we extinguished it.

He dropped the shovel and glared at me, a mixture of disgust, anger, and fear, contorting his grizzled features. "I fucking told you to be careful. I'm not gonna tell you again. You do this when it's raining. Light it again and I quit. I mean it."

Normandy didn't have to tell me again. And I didn't light it again, until one day when it was pissing rain. I could tell by the look on his face he'd suffered a nasty experience with fire. Someone close to him had died. Burned to death.

Nobody had to tell me. I just knew.

A sound. A twig snapping. Or was it crackling? Or was it popping? Whatever it was, it snapped me out of my reflection. Suddenly, I thought I could smell smoke. I stood up quickly, realizing with a sense of anguish I had not gone down to the beach site this morning to check last night's fire, in spite of last night's nightmare. Somehow I'd gotten distracted and frittered away the hours playing on social media, binge-watching the news, and reading Ray Bradbury's *Fahrenheit 451. Yikes, of all things to read now.*

Opening the screen door quickly, I shuddered, reaching for my flashlight and baseball cap. A million thoughts, like a million flashing fireflies, were dancing through my mind. *Is it too late? Is the fire raging? Why didn't I check it today? Am I gonna to die? Are my friends and neighbors gonna burn? Have I pushed the envelope one step too far with Mother Nature? Hell hath no fury like Mother Nature's scorn.*

My mother's warning reverberated in my head: *"You play with fire, son, and you will get burned. It's not a question of if, it's when."*

I was gripped by a tingly, adrenaline-fueled paranoia that I was coming to an end, that the world was coming to an end. Beads of sweat popped on my forehead in rapid succession and streaked down my face.

I climbed into my pickup, started it, revved the engine, and veered toward the winding road leading to the beach. By the time I arrived, I was in a state of almost complete and utter panic. Even as I approached the fire pit, I could see an orange glow surrounding the area. I quickly parked the truck, killed the engine, climbed out, scrambled over to the fire pit, and shone the flashlight beam down upon it. Orange embers glowed and small spirals of smoke twirled up. But the night was calm. It wasn't going anywhere. It would be out on its own in a matter of hours. Maybe less.

I sighed deeply, looking around the site, feeling my heart rate slowly but surely returning to something approximating normal. I set my flashlight down, picked up a wooden poker and jabbed at the hot embers, trying to convince myself my eyes weren't deceiving me. But, no. Just a few hot embers and a few twirling ribbons of smoke. I carefully placed the poker on a log near the fire, careful not to put the hot end on any loose twigs.

A crackling sound startled me. I jumped, jerking my head toward the beachfront, obscured partially by a seventy-foot tree bluff. Then I saw it. An orange glow near the water's edge—about six feet off the ground, right smack in the middle of a three-foot diameter tree, fanning out along the tree branches into the night sky and wreaking destruction on everything it touched. An apocalypse. Armageddon. Just like my nightmare. Seized by panic, I grabbed the flashlight and charged to the water's edge. About ten feet before the blaze, I stopped, the realization of the reality of what I was witnessing striking me like a bucket of cold water upside the head.

It was the moon rising up above the ocean, looming large, a fiery orange ball peering through the trees.

"Get your shit together," I said, taking several deep breaths in an attempt to replace déjà vu with reality.

That crackling sound. Again. I looked around, trying to determine its origin. Nothing. I looked out to sea, taking in the magnificence and stunning beauty of the moon rising above the water. Then I saw it. A large bank of dark rainclouds rolling toward shore. The crackling again. But this time I knew what it was. It wasn't the snap, crackle, pop of a fire. It was the bone-cracking sound of thunder.

Like a bowling ball rolling down the bowling lanes of hell, it came again, this time loud, jarring, and unmistakable. Then lightning streaked across the sky, touched down on the sea about a hundred feet from shore, and exploded into a ball of flames that danced along the wavy water before fizzling into nothingness. Then I heard the pitter-patter of light rain that soon turned torrential. Sheets of windblown rain driving toward the shoreline. It was all I could do to flee. By the time I got to my pickup, I was drenched from head to toe. I started it, turned the wipers on high, and began to slowly and cautiously navigate the winding, uphill road to my house.

Sheets of rain pounded the truck, obscuring my vision. The sky flared with lightning. One lightning bolt struck the narrow dirt beach road and exploded into the ground. Thunder boomed in the heavens. I pumped the brakes and came to a stop a few feet from the lightning missile and watched, horrified, as a small explosion directly in front of me blasted a large pot hole in the road, spraying dirt high in the sky and drenching the pickup.

"Holy fucking shit," I said as I watched the windshield quickly become obscured by muddy streaks. The windshield wiper on the driver side got wedged between some rocks and a large mud-packed mound of dirt. I climbed out of the truck and swept my hand and arm across the windshield, removing most of it and then scrambling around to the passenger side to repeat the procedure. After I finished, I quickly examined the hole: About five feet wide and about two feet deep. By now, there were rivers of water flowing down the road toward the beach, and I wondered if I would even be able to make it home.

I spun around, heading for the ajar driver door and slipped, face-planting the road with a splash, and getting up covered in mud and barely able to see six inches in front of me. The rain came harder. The thunder intensified. Lightning struck in the distance, and from my muddied peripheral vision I saw another small fireball erupt somewhere nearby in the forest. I prayed the rain would put it out as I felt for the door handle, pulled myself toward the truck, and climbed in.

Inside, I reached into the back seat, found an old towel, and wiped my muddy face. When I could see, I locked up the four-wheel-drive, drove warily through the large crater in front of me, and proceeded slowly back to the house.

About two thirds of the way home, I stopped the truck, knowing with a dread certainty that what I was seeing was no moon. Even though the vehicle windows were closed, I could smell a nauseating and pungent odor of smoke. There was a bright orange glow, vaguely resembling a macabre halo, about five hundred feet directly in front of me. Panicking for the third time that day, I gunned the truck, slithering up the road in a metal casket heading straight for an inferno.

And when I arrived at the clearing, my worst nightmares were realized. What was once my house was now an orange fireball, large flames licking defiantly into the dark sky and the torrential rain.

I watched, terrified, as a lightning bolt exploded out of the blackness above, struck my barn and shattered a large section of the roof. Asphalt shingles and wood debris rained down as the barn burst into flames.

A flaming two-by-four landed on the hood of the truck and I backed up, dislodged it, and plowed forward, racing to the end of the driveway that fronted the highway, stopping and looking back sadly at what was once a peaceful, humble and secluded abode. It was now a mass of angry flames. I didn't much like fire anymore at that moment.

My mind raced. My cell phone, my identification, my credit cards. Where were they? Then I remembered. I'd put them in the glove box the night before after driving straight down to the beach after a pre-party booze run. I popped open the glove box and there they were. *Thank God. Thank Mother Nature. Thank someone for small miracles.*

I grabbed the cell phone and tried to call 911. *Dead battery. Fuck.* Fear-induced adrenaline coursing through my body, I pulled out onto the highway, toward small-town Murray River, where I knew I could enlist someone at the town Esso to call the fire department. Five minutes away in clement weather. In this mess, maybe fifteen.

Wipers on full, I cautiously drove into the blackness. No real point in gunning it and risking my life. There was no saving the house now, no saving the barn. The only thing I wanted to save now was Mother Nature, animals, and people. But she seemed intent on destroying my home, destroying herself, destroying anything and everything. Was I next? Had my disrespect reached the point of zero tolerance? A morbid thought burst into my mind as I navigated the two-lane highway in near-zero visibility: *How many bullets does Mother Nature have in the chamber? And is she saving the last one for me?*

In that instant, I was blinded by a flash of light. A lightning bolt struck the hood of the truck, exploded into a hissing fireball, and catapulted the fiery metal casket into the air. White knuckles gripping the steering wheel, I watched catatonic with fear as my world spun upside down. Metal grated along wet pavement and sparks flew as the truck flipped on its hood, skidded toward the ditch, and plummeted to the bottom of the seven-foot ditch. I felt a flash of sharp pain as my head struck something solid. Consciousness ebbed and flowed as white stars danced around. I blinked repeatedly, trying to stay conscious. I could smell gasoline. Oil. Smoke. I felt the cab heating up, a barbeque with human flesh on the griddle. *Do you want that extra crispy, ma'am?* Flames began licking up the cracked, rain-drenched windshield. It was only a matter of time before the vehicle would explode. I wiped the top of my head. A large bump. Warm blood. My vision blurred and a wave of nausea swept over me.

Do something. Get the hell out of here. For a moment, calmness enveloped my senses. A sort of dreamy resignation. Or was it resolve? I remembered an article I had read once explaining the fight-or-flight response. How some people, in the face of life-threatening danger, flee in a panic; while others develop super-human strength and fight their way to safety. What would I do? Fight and flight were inextricably linked. I had to fight my way out of the truck to take flight. Could I do it?

I reached for my seatbelt as my body began pulsating with energy and my mind began miraculously clearing—the built-in human self-preservation mechanisms booting up. I unclasped the seatbelt in a smooth motion, wrapped two hands tightly around the door handle, and tugged. Nothing. I tugged again.

Click.

It opened. In a moment of extreme lucidity, I grabbed my wallet and dead phone, tucking both in my top pocket, spun around and crawled through a narrow passageway of flames to what was surely safety. A second chance. A life preserved, so that I might revisit Mother Nature with a new air of respect and admiration.

Boom. A loud explosion. I flew out of the ditch, and landed hard on asphalt. I felt another lump growing above my right eye as I tried to get up, faltered, and tumbled head-first onto asphalt. The lights, my lights, dimmed. I watched as a small circle of burning debris a few inches from my face faded from orange to gray, then gray to black. Black nothingness that seemed to last for hours. Then a bright white angelic figure loomed large in front of my floating body. I knew who she was.

"Mother Nature," I croaked.

"Yes," she said with a look of deep sadness and compassion. "You have to be more careful. You should have been more careful."

"I will next time. I promise... "

***

Exactly eight minutes later, a blaring firetruck stopped in the middle of a rain-swept highway along with an ambulance and two cops cars.

The volunteer fire chief climbed out of the truck and approached the body stretched out in the middle of the road. One leg jutted out at an awkward angle, clearly broken. The man's head was a strange mixture of rainwater, mud, and blood; and what the fire chief thought might be brain matter.

Two paramedics rushed to the scene, one bending down straightaway and checking for a pulse.

"Is he dead?" the fire chief asked.

"He's got a pulse," the paramedic said, waving to his stretcher-wheeling partner. "But it's a weak one."

The Succubus

Jeremy Hildebrandt didn't completely understand what was happening to him at first. But he went along with it. At least his little head did. His fully erect little head. He was in a foreign land perched in the nosebleed section of a baseball field. Or was it a soccer field? He wasn't sure. But he was sure the Asian beauty he'd been ogling a few minutes ago had saddled up on top of him, blinked a few times with dark puppy dog eyes, and said, "I'm tired." Then she'd leaned back, curling up in his arms, her head and long black hair resting on his chest, and closed her eyes.

Now, she was slowly moving her hand along his leg, closer and closer to his little head, or what his Vancouver buddies often referred to as the little general, who had a habit of commanding the troops, or a tiny soldier as it were, way beyond enemy lines.

Jeremy sighed, wondering if he should chance it. Put his hand on her bare, trim, tight belly and caress his way up to her gravity-defying breasts. *Why the hell not?*

He touched her belly and she moaned softly. Her skin was hot to the touch. He began a slow, circling motion toward her bosom, pleasurable moans escaping her lips with every inch of progress.

She ran her hand over his shorts, lightly, teasingly brushing against his tent pole.

"Ohhh," he said. "That feels good."

Out of nowhere, a man appeared. Looming large. Cropped hair. Shadowy. Dark squinting eyes. "Hey, Sulina. What are you doing there?" His voice was booming and authoritative.

"I'm just sleeping, honey." Her voice was melodious, sweet, and sexy. Unperturbed.

Less agitated, he said, "Who are you sleeping with?"

A hint of fear pricked the hairs on the back of Jeremy's neck. He removed his hand from her belly, *probably a little too late*, he thought. He then leaned his head to one side and closed his eyes. It was all he could think of to do. He suddenly felt exhausted.

That same sweet and sexy voice. "He's just a friend, honey. A good friend."

A long and stifling silence.

"All right," the man said finally. "But don't do anything I wouldn't do."

"Don't you worry about that," the woman said. "Now, run along."

Jeremy cocked an eye, just enough to see the shadowy image of the man spin around and vanish.

The woman kissed him gently on the cheek.

Tingling sensations poured through his body, down to his throbbing manhood. He grinned, opening both eyes. "Who's... who's he?"

"Just a friend," the woman said. "A good friend."

The mutual caressing resumed, the wild exploration of erogenous zones. Several dozen moans of pleasure later, just when Jeremy was about to explode, he opened his eyes. His heart pounded in his chest, his member twitched spasmodically, and he scanned the room, taking in the four dreary walls of his shitty apartment. His member shriveled into a sticky wet noodle instantly and he let out a deep sigh of despair.

"Fuck, did that feel real." *But, no it was only a dream and pretty damn close to being a wet one at that.*

What was real was Jeremy's shitty little life. At 36, he was still a virgin. He was awkward and nerdy with women and in all his years of existence had only managed one date. And that was the high school graduation dance, a long time ago, to be sure. And it had ended with Jeremy drinking a mickey of rum, vomiting all over his baby-blue suit, and his date's elegant white gown.

Disaster. The laughing stock of the high school.

What else? He had a go-nowhere-fast job as a landscaper. Horticulturist. Team player. Opportunity for advancement. Higher pay for the right candidate. That's how it had been advertised. But what it amounted to was a crappy position cutting lawns for $13.00 per hour. It sucked.

Jeremy couldn't even afford a car. And on that wage, he could barely afford his second-story, one-bedroom apartment on downtown Hastings Street in Vancouver. Skid road. Here lived the highest population per square inch of drug addicts, criminals, prostitutes, homeless, crazies, and otherwise marginalized members of society than virtually anywhere on the planet.

The Sewer, as some liked to call it. Jeremy had been flushed down the toilet of life and lived a shitty, pathetic, and sad existence in the Sewer.

He got out of bed slowly as the weight of his bitter reality settled over him. He slalomed around empty beer cans and pizza boxes and into the bathroom. He relieved himself, caught a glimpse of his wild eyes and mop of brown hair in the mirror, and looked away. He didn't want to face his mug today.

Determined not to look, he ran the cold water and splashed a couple of handfuls of it on his face. He grabbed a towel and, wiping his face, emerged into the living room, and sat down on a tattered couch. Yelling, screaming, and thumping, from above. Paper-thin walls. His neighbors, Jennie and Jamie, sure as shit drunker than skunks, had already started their daily alcohol-fueled fight. Jeremy glanced at the clock. 9:30 am. *Wow. They're starting early this Saturday. Usually by 11:30, they're pie-eyed and pounding the shit out of one another.*

Traffic hissed outside on the street below, intermingled with echoes of the desperate and down and out. Jeremy picked up a pair of foam earplugs from a cluttered coffee table and inserted them into his ears. Jennie and Jamie could kill themselves for all he cared right now. Jeremy closed his eyes, wanting to escape it all, go back to that baseball field, or soccer field, or whatever the fuck it was.

That hot woman. Her touch. So real. He'd dreamt before obviously, even a few sticky ones. But nothing like this. This woman came to him in his time of need to save him from Loserville. Show him once and for all that, yes, he was capable of having a relationship. Women *did* like him. Women *do* like him. He wasn't a nerd after all. He was a fucking stud. He was sure of it.

This called for some research. As he flipped open his laptop, he heard a loud knock, above the earplugs. They were pretty good at filtering sound, but far from perfect. He plucked them out and stared at the door, wide-eyed, a chill suddenly sweeping over him.

The knocks continued. *Bang, bang, bang.*

What, do you think the door will answer itself? Nimrod. Tool. Stop it, and answer the door.

He approached the door. "Who is it?"

A muffled voice. "It's me, idiot. You forget about our breakfast plans?"

***

Dipping an oily piece of toast into a fried egg at Bert's, a greasy spoon restaurant just on the fringe of Skid Road, Jeremy looked up at Carl Milt, a work buddy, and tried to figure out why he had such a silly grin on his face. After all, Carl was only one step removed from Jeremy's precarious grip on survival. Sure, Carl owned a car, but he also lived rent-free in his mother's basement. If that didn't spell loser, Jeremy didn't know what did. Although Jeremy might be in the same boat if his mother and father would allow it. But after he'd dropped out of college, refusing to follow his father's prearranged plan for him, he'd been unceremoniously kicked out of his parent's house and told by his old man, "When you get your shit together, give us a call. It's called tough love." That was seven years ago. He hadn't called his parents since, and after some of their messages had gone unanswered, a long chasm of lonely and self-pitying silence had followed. But Jeremy wasn't thinking about that now. No. He was thinking of how he almost got laid last night.

He couldn't help a small delicious smile at the thought of that hottie. Never mind. He was getting distracted again.

"Why are you looking at me like that?" he asked Carl.

Carl, a behemoth of a man, pawed his grizzled chin, his grin widening. Powdery toast crumbs dotted his white t-shirt. "You look like you got laid last night," Carl said. "Did you?"

Jeremy knew Carl had enough porn magazines in his tiny rent-free flat to fill the Library of Congress. He also knew women wanted nothing to do with the fat slob. "What do you mean?"

"It's a simple question."

No point hiding anything, Jeremy thought. Maybe he could get some answers. "I didn't get laid, but I almost did."

"You met someone?"

"Yeah."

"Do tell."

"It's not like you think. I... I met someone last night. In my dreams."

Carl guffawed loudly and a few restaurant patrons gawked. Looks of annoyance, even fear on a few faces. "In your dreams. That's fucking classic."

"Fuck you. If you're gonna laugh, I won't tell you."

"I was just kidding. Come on. I was just laughing at the play on words. You know, in your dreams. Get it?"

"I get it and I ain't fucking laughing."

"Was it a wet dream?"

A few heads turned. Looks of interest.

"Keep your voice down."

Carl leaned in and whispered, "Sorry, buddy. I'd like to hear it. Really."

Jeremy waited until most of the motley-looking patrons returned to their food, returned to their boring conversations, returned to their mundane lives. An overweight and slovenly couple entered, took a booth behind them, and began chattering loudly. Two patrons got up, paid their bill at the cashier, and left. Jeremy was happy for the loud chatter. It would provide some cover.

Jeremy told the story, omitting the part about being on the brink of an explosive orgasm.

But Carl figured it out. "Did you blow your load?"

"Almost, man. But the thing is, it felt so real. That ever happen to you?"

"No, but I sure as fuck wish it would. And I think I know what happened."

"You do? Do tell."

"You ever heard of the succubus?"

"No."

"A succubus is a female demon, or some people think a supernatural entity that doesn't have evil intentions. It enters men's dreams and seduces them. I've read a lot about it. Some men claim to have married their succubus after some pretty fucking erotic sex sessions. Left their wives and everything. I'm talking amazing blow jobs, anal, you fucking name it. Really kinky shit. The male version is called the incubus. Are you sure it wasn't a lady-boy trying to seduce you?"

Jeremy flushed. "No, it wasn't a fucking lady-boy." He lowered his voice to a whisper. "I massaged her... clit. Fingered her pussy." He decided a little more teasing wouldn't hurt. A little revenge. "And it was dripping like Niagara Falls."

Jeremy grinned, shit-eating, as he saw a frown tighten Carl's lips together. *He's jealous. That'll teach you for the lady-boy comment. Motherfucker.*

Carl's expression grew serious. "Hey, if you ever find a way to bring her into the real world, or maybe she's in the real world already and you just need to find a way to meet her, do me a favor, bro, and ask her if she has any friends. I'm tired of beating off to porn mags and internet porn. I want a real woman, man."

Jeremy couldn't resist the jab. More revenge. "Did you say you want a real man?"

The sadness on Carl's face deepened. Jeremy could've sworn he saw Carl's eyes moisten a little.

"Come on, man," Carl said. "I was just joking about the lady-boy comment. Besides, I know *you* don't, but some people like it like that. There's nothing wrong with it. You know what I meant. Help me out if you can."

"Sorry," Jeremy said, feeling guilty and sorry for his friend. After all, they were both in the same loser canoe, floating down shit creek without paddles. Except Jeremy had a paddle now and he had a renewed determination to transform the muddy waters of shit creek into a clear-running, honey-flavored, gushing river, overflowing with succubus love juices. *Niagara Falls!*

***

Jeremy felt a soft touch on his arm and opened his eyes. It was pitch-black, with zero visibility. He could smell her. Honey and roses. He knew who she was. He reached for her with both hands.

"It's you. My succubus. Thank God you're back."

"I'm Delilah," she said softly. Her voice was distant.

"Delilah, come to me."

"I'll do more than come to you."

Jeremy got the sexual innuendo, felt it in his stirring loins. He was tingling with excitement and anticipation. He stood up, groping around in the darkness. "Where... where are you?"

"Oh, but you'll see me when I want you to see me," Delilah said. "Until then, you'll feel me."

Jeremy felt a hand expertly unzip his fly, grasp his throbbing member, and begin to pump. In less than a minute, he exploded with a violent orgasm.

When his body stopped shaking and his breathing returned to normal, he said, "Thank you, Delilah. I want you in my life... permanently."

The voice distant, a little colder: "Careful what you wish for."

But a desperate Jeremy pressed on. "I don't care what it takes. I'll do anything. I want you in my life. In the real world. What will you have me do?"

"Oh, but this is the real world. And this isn't all about you."

Jeremy remembered. Carl. Carl needs help. Carl asked for help. Carl asked for a succubus. He didn't know how to put it discreetly. "My friend, Carl. He needs to get laid. Do you have a female friend?"

"I have many female friends. Goddesses."

"Will you send one to Carl?"

"I'll do your bidding, but are you sure that's what you want?"

"It's what he wants. He asked me. Is there a downside to this?"

"That's in the eye of the beholder," Delilah said.

"What does that mean?"

"It means what you want it to mean."

She's speaking in riddles. No straight answers. Do I really want to go through with this? But it didn't take long for flashbacks of his own dismal life and Carl's abysmal life to tip the scales. "If I tell you to send him a succubus, will you be with me for the rest of my life?"

"That's the first step, my dear. Only the first step."

"Okay, send Carl a goddess succubus."

"Done."

Jeremy immediately began having second thoughts. His id was running the show. "Are you really a succubus? A demon?"

"I am a manifestation of your dark side. I am the incarnation of all of your sexual fantasies. To know yourself, you have to know your dark side. To embrace yourself, you have to embrace your dark side."

A sudden flash of light appeared in front of Jeremy, and in that light, he caught a glimpse of Delilah's golden breasts, outstretched and over-sized nipples, attentive and rock-hard. They were like large red eyes, boring into his soul and drilling down on all of his insecurities. His apprehensions melted like hot candle wax.

"I'll embrace my dark side. I want you... I want all of you... now!"

***

Strange, Jeremy thought. At noon the following Sunday, he couldn't reach Carl. Three phone calls. Three voice mail messages. Now he was beginning to panic. *What the fuck did I do?*

Bang... bang, bang, bang. Loud knocks on the door.

Jeremy's nerves were frayed—loose electrical wires, jiggling around zapping and popping on the street after a terrible storm.

"Who is it?" he said louder and with more tension in his tone than he'd intended.

"Detective Warner. Open the door, please." Loud. Authoritative. Angry.

Breaking out in a sweat, Jeremy rushed to the door and opened it a crack. A red-haired, red-bearded man flashed a badge. "Open up. I just wanna have a few words with you."

Jeremy opened the door.

Jeremy sat down on the cluttered couch as Detective Warner studied the surroundings, unable to hide a flash of disgust. He chose to stand, towering above Jeremy. He couldn't be more intimidating.

"You Jeremy Hildebrandt?"

"Yeah," Jeremy said, knowing full well the man already knew the answer to that question.

"Where were you last night?"

"At home." *Shouldn't I be asking why?*

"Anyone who can vouch for that?"

Jeremy remembered bumping into Jennie and Jamie in the hallway last night before he'd turned in for the night. They were streaking down the hallway, semi-naked, chasing each other with broken beer bottles—in the heat of battle. He'd threatened to call the cops and they'd disappeared, but not before several profanity-laden threats. Would they even vouch for him? But it was all he had.

"I'm pretty sure my neighbors will vouch for me." Jeremy wasn't at all sure. "Why? What's this all about? Why do I need an alibi?"

The detective brushed a few newspapers off a ratty lounge chair, dusted it off with a hand, and sat. "Your friend, Carl Milt, died last night."

Jeremy's mouth dropped open. "What?"

"That's right, he's dead."

"How...how did he die?"

"You don't know?"

"I wouldn't be asking if I knew. My God, that's terrible." Jeremy brought both hands to his face and slumped over on the couch, feeling the tears come streaming down through his fingers.

The detective watched stone-faced.

Three minutes later, Jeremy sat up, wiped the tears away, and looked straight at Detective Warner. "How did he die? And for fuck sakes, don't sit here and tell me you think I had anything to do with it."

"Actually, it's not a bad way to go, you ask me. No disrespect intended. From our evidence so far, it looks like your friend was fucked to death. Semen stains all over his sheets and bed, covers in complete disarray, and one single broken bedside lamp. Otherwise no signs of a struggle, and an oddly purple penis. We're still waiting for a coroner's report to determine the exact cause of death, but it looks very much like he fucked so hard and fast he ended up pushing himself to the point of extreme physical exertion and succumbed to a heart attack."

Succumbed... succumbed to the succubus. I did this. Oh fuck!

"Are you okay?" Detective Warner asked. "You've gone as white as a sheet of paper. Or an arrest warrant."

"I'm not okay," Jeremy said, exhaling deeply. "Carl was a good friend of mine."

"Was he? When was the last time you saw him?"

Jeremy suspected the detective probably already knew. "We had breakfast yesterday at Bert's. It's our Saturday ritual."

"And how did that go?"

Jeremy was torn. Torn between telling the cop the truth about unleashing the succubus yet worried that this truth would both brand him a lunatic, pointing more fingers at him potentially, and ruin his chances with the fantasy woman of his dreams. He decided to sugar-coat it. "Fine. The usual. Carl works... worked with me and a lot of it was shop talk about our job."

"Landscapers as I understand it?"

"Right."

"Did Carl mention anything about a woman in his life?"

"He said he wants one in his life. But Carl hasn't had a woman in his life for as long as I can remember."

"No female friends?"

"Not that I know of."

"And you weren't trying to help him out of his predicament?"

How does he know that? He doesn't. He's fishing. Stick to your story. "No. I couldn't if I wanted to. I haven't had a woman in my life for as long as I can remember."

"No female friends?"

"Not really."

"What does that mean?"

"No."

"Do you know of anyone who might want to harm Carl? Any enemies?"

"No one comes to mind."

The detective's phone rang. He scowled at the incoming number and silenced the ringing by pressing a button. "Fucking city's going to hell in a handbasket."

But at least I'm enjoying the ride, Jeremy thought. *At least I'm enjoying the ride.*

"I gotta go," the detective said. He stood and tossed a business card on the coffee table. "That's my number. I'll probably want to ask you a few more questions down the road if that's okay."

Jeremy nodded.

"And if you can think of anything at all, no matter how insignificant you think it might be, don't hesitate to call me."

"I will," Jeremy lied. He wanted this man the hell out of his apartment and the hell out of his life.

***

He'd read the online newspaper accounts. He'd watched the TV news coverage of the incident. He'd wracked his brain with a million different scenarios of why he wasn't at fault. But nothing he did or said to himself could assuage the guilt he was feeling.

He sat on a log at Locarno Beach, watching the sun set on the crimson horizon. Most of the beach-goers had disappeared, but there were still a few loiterers; the odd couple strolling arm in arm; a woman pushing her toddler along the shoreline in a baby carriage; two male teenagers on a nearby log, sipping from a paper-wrapped bottle and occasionally giggling drunkenly or making some stupid comment.

Jeremy was oblivious. He was engaged in a fierce battle with inner (perhaps some outer ones as well) demons and moral conscience. The inner demons claimed he had nothing to do with Carl's death. He was only trying to help his friend. It wasn't his fault a succubus had fucked him to death. And maybe that was not what had really happened. Maybe, as the news media liked to obtusely say, *"There is no there there." What a dumb saying.*

Maybe the succubus was just a myth—a figment of a sex-and-love-starved and, yes, damaged psyche. The product of years and years of loneliness, self-loathing, and boredom.

However, regardless of his attempts at mitigation and justification, a deep sadness permeated every fiber of Jeremy's being; in part because his moral conscience held a different view, one that painted a macabre picture of Delilah as a viscerally real instrument of the devil. A demon who had seduced Jeremy in his moment of weakness and used him as a conduit for evil. Didn't that make him an accessory to murder? Or, in this day and age, an actual murderer. *You don't have to pull the trigger to be convicted of murder. You just have to order the hit. I didn't order any hit, goddammit. I was only trying to help. Were you really? Yours was a self-serving agenda to be with Delilah.*

"No, no, no... I didn't do it."

"Do you want some?"

Jeremy jumped, removing his hands from his face, and looking up. Back-dropped against a stunning setting sun stood a young man with a mop of curly black hair and a paper-wrapped bottle.

"You look like you could use it," the man said, kneeling down and thrusting the bottle in Jeremy's face.

"What's... what's in it?"

"Jack Daniels sipping whiskey. Cures all mankind's problems. At least for tonight."

Jeremy grabbed the bottle quickly and took two long pulls. The warm stinging sensation that washed down his throat and into his tummy felt good. It was just what he needed right now.

"Thanks," he said, returning the bottle to its owner. "I needed that."

The proverbial tip of the iceberg.

***

Liberally swilling a brand-new paper-wrapped bottle of Jack Daniels in his run-down apartment later that evening, he stumbled around looking for a sign—any sign at all that perhaps Delilah was real. He started with his crusty bedsheets, sniffing around for any scent of women's perfume, trying to detect the tell-tale honey-and-roses scent.

But, no. Only a strong sweaty odor and the faint smell of ammonia. He rose from the bed, went to his closet, and pulled open the door. Clothes on hangers. Clothes on the floor. Some dirty. Some clean. He bent down and started rummaging around, hoping to find a pair of women's panties, a bra, any article of women's clothing that would trigger the faint-hope clause. Nothing.

As he was closing the door, something caught his eye—the magnified grizzled face of his late friend, Carl Milt. His blood-red eyes glowed ominously. His mouth hung open in an expression of unadulterated horror.

"No," Jeremy said, slamming the closet door, rushing from the bedroom, slamming the bedroom door, and plopping down on the living room couch.

He pulled long and hard on the Jack Daniels, wiping some spillage from his chin. "It's not you, Carl. You're not here. It wasn't me."

A thunderous voice: "You killed me! Why did you kill me?"

"No, no, and fucking no! I didn't kill you! I was trying to help you!" Jeremy closed his eyes and gritted his teeth. He tried to conjure up an image of Delilah. He wanted some relief from the overpowering guilt. None came.

He sat there for several minutes listening to his erratic heartbeat and trying to calm troubled waters. An idea occurred to him. He put the liquor bottle down, raced into the bedroom, and opened the closet door. "Carl... Carl. Are you in there?"

Only rumpled clothes.

He slowly lifted a wrinkled shirt, jumping back when he felt something on his hand. Claws. Warmth. A mouse squeaked and sprinted out of his closet, quickly finding refuge underneath his bed.

He ignored it. "Carl. I'm sorry. I only wanted to help you. I was selfish and foolish, but you asked me. Remember? You asked me. You wanted to get laid... wanted a woman in your life."

His thoughts returned to Delilah, and he returned to the living room and to drinking. As he polished off half the bottle and felt the comforting and calming effects of alcohol sweeping away his worries, he stared at the lone window in his apartment. It was blocked with a black blanket, a makeshift curtain. There was a small triangular gap at the bottom right-hand corner where a sphere of light radiated in from the streetlights outside. As he continued to focus on it, it slowly grew and then transformed into the seductive body of a woman, naked, except for a pair of red dental-floss panties.

He watched in awe as Delilah's soft features materialized; her long and beautiful mane; golden soul-searching eyes; soft and tender facial features.

He tried to stand but wobbled and plopped back down on his ass. "It's you... it's really you."

"You can save Carl," she said softly. "And have me."

Jeremy's eyes narrowed as he fought the tent rising in his jeans. "He's dead. You killed him."

"No, he's not dead. He's in a better place. But he needs your help to pass fully into the other side. You know what you need to do."

As Jeremy began to protest, Delilah's long, slender arm elongated, reaching his manhood in a heartbeat and tugging on it gently. The stirrings of desire erupted like an oil-gushing geyser and Delilah disappeared.

Jeremy's resolve dissolved. He knew what he had to do.

Fifteen minutes later, he surveyed the darkness and despair of his apartment and of his life. He took a swill of liquid courage and grinned maniacally. He set the bottle on a nearby table and went to work. Using a long serrated-edged knife, he carved a hole in the ceiling about the size of a baseball. He ignored bits of plaster falling on his head and shoulders. He pulled out a chunk of plaster and tossed it on the floor. He dusted off the two-inch diameter pipe underneath, tied the rope around it securely, and placed the noose end over his neck. His body began shaking as he tightened the noose. Tears began streaming down his face. He picked up the bottle, gulped down a few more mouthfuls, and cleared his throat.

He reflected on his life and what it had amounted to. It didn't take him too long to realize it hadn't amounted to shit. His relationships—except his relationship with Carl and Delilah—hadn't amounted to shit.

"I hope you're right, Delilah. I hope I'm going to a better place. I hope what you said is true—that I can save Carl... that I can have you forever. This fucking world doesn't owe me anything and I don't owe it anything."

He cinched the noose up until he felt the hemp strands biting into his neck and aggravating flesh. Rope burn. He drained the bottle and whipped it at the window. The black curtain absorbed the blow and it clattered to the floor.

"Cruel world, you can fuck off and die." He kicked out the chair he stood on. He felt his full 180 pounds drop and get abruptly halted by the noose. It tightened quickly. He gasped for breath. He heard a heart-wrenching snapping sound. He coughed and whiskey-laced spittle dribbled from his mouth.

Gray faded to black and he drew his last breath.

***

Jeremy woke up out of sorts in a dungeon-like hallway. He heard disturbing screams and shouts intermingled with moans and groans of pleasure. Occasionally, maniacal cackling laughter punctuated the cacophony of sounds. He tried to make sense of his surroundings. Cold, gray brick walls. A series of long and winding hallways, lit by dangling red light bulbs. A series of doors every fifty feet or so. He patted his face. It felt real but cold and damp. He ran a finger along his neck and it smarted from rope burns. He also felt ligature marks.

He got up off the cold, damp floor, selected a corridor randomly, and began walking. High-pitched shrieks stopped him at the first door. He opened it. In the middle of a room resembling a torture chamber, a nude woman lay on her back. Her ankles and wrists were rope-bound. She struggled futilely as dozens of dwarf-sized men fondled her breasts, fingered her pussy. One stood above her, jacking off above her head, grinning from ear to ear.

She turned to Jeremy, eyes wide with horror. "Help me!!"

A dwarf stuck his dick in her mouth and muffled her attempts at saying more. The dwarf turned to Jeremy and motioned with a finger. "Come and get some."

A dose of adrenaline exploded in Jeremy's heart and he quickly shook his head. Four dwarfs leaped off the table and charged toward him, one wielding a butcher knife.

Jeremy slammed the door and hurried down the corridor. Moans of pleasure stopped him at door number two. He pulled. It opened on squeaky hinges. Inside, it was lit with numerous candles that surrounded a large plush black couch. In front of the couch, a large ornate stone coffee table, accessorized with a wide variety of sex toys. A beautiful, naked woman lay on the couch sipping a drink from a golden goblet. A tiny red line of liquid dribbled down her chin as she finished a sip and smiled seductively at Jeremy. A large muscular man had his head buried between her legs. He slurped and slopped. The woman set the drink down, thrust her head back, and began to moan some more.

The man withdrew his head from her crotch and turned to Jeremy. His face was blood-red. Horns protruded from his head. He wiped a milky-white substance from his face and grinned devilishly, a mouth full of horse teeth. "Do you want some, young man?"

"Maybe later," Jeremy said, closing the door quickly and moving on to door number three, where he heard voices. He put his ear to the door.

"Oww... that fucking hurts. Please, please... "

The voice was unmistakable. Carl. Now was his chance to free his friend. The reward, Delilah. Adrenaline still fueling his fire, he pulled hard on the door handle with both hands. After some effort, it squeaked halfway open.

He rushed inside and stopped in the middle of the dimly lit room, mouth agape at what beheld him. A completely naked Carl was chained to a wall. Blood trickled down his chest from a series of small cuts. Whip lashes.

A statuesque woman dressed in a tight black bodysuit stood a few feet away. She whipped him repeatedly with a long, blood-drenched horse-whip. Each time she snapped the tip into his chest, a new gash would appear and ooze blood. With each snap of the whip, Carl would wince and cry out in pain. However, his erect purple penis told a different story.

Jeremy moved quickly and grabbed the tip of the whip as the dominatrix arched her back for another devastating strike. He pulled it from her hands and backed up against the wall. She spun around and, yelling obscenities, angrily advanced upon him.

"Stop," Carl said. "Sit down and shut up."

She put her snake-like tail between her legs and dropped into a plush brown leather couch beside another woman draped in a golden blanket.

Carl grinned at Jeremy. "I knew you'd come."

Jeremy's eyes darted back and forth for a few seconds—couch, Carl, couch, Carl, couch... finally settling on Carl. "I'm here to save you."

"Save me from what?" Carl asked. "Some people like it like this."

Jeremy was incredulous and confused simultaneously. "You mean you want this? You're okay with this?"

Carl nodded. "It was my turn to be submissive. But you broke the spell by taking the whip." He turned to the dominatrix, who had begun to lift the golden veil of silence from the woman next to her.

"Get me out of these chains, bitch," Carl said. "Now!"

The dominatrix hurried over to Carl and began unchaining him.

Delilah, her smooth, naked body glistening in the suffused red light, sprang from beneath the golden blanket, snatched the whip out of Jeremy's hands, and wrapped him in a tight embrace. She slid her forked tongue deep into his mouth, sucking and slurping.

He hugged and kissed her ravenously until he almost choked on her serpent-like tongue.

Spitting it out, he looked into her dark, vacant, and emotionless eyes. "I thought I had to save Carl to be with you forever."

She cackled cynically. "The only person you had to save was yourself... and you couldn't even do that right."

Fake Friends

"Fake friends," Michael MacDonald said to a dark and empty house. "That's all they are."

He'd just arrived at his inner-city Calgary home after leaving a dinner party. He'd been an invited guest of Mila and Dennis Steinweister, his friends. At least they called themselves friends. Three months earlier, he'd gifted them a paperback copy of his new novel, practically begging them to read it and post a review on Amazon. At that time, they'd seemed interested, asking Michael to summarize it.

He'd spent weeks polishing the short synopsis and proudly repeated it: "Mysterious and terrifying attacks by the Shadow People and the Hat Man lead a nightmare-plagued man to suspect an enigmatic doctor has accidentally opened a portal to hell."

They'd both promised to read *The Dark Presence* and post reviews if they liked it.

Leading up to the dinner party, Michael had tried to keep his expectations in check. He kept repeating the wise stoic philosophy: "Expect nothing, for thou shalt not be disappointed."

The Dark Presence had already garnered many rave reviews from book-buyers whom he didn't even know and hadn't even solicited. Five-star reviews, many from readers who'd said they couldn't put it down until they'd finished it. Shouldn't that be enough? Maybe, but it was nice to get a little support from your friends. Nice to know they took an interest in your passion and would give you a little positive feedback and encouragement once in a while. A little validation for all your blood, sweat, and tears.

But that's not what had happened a few hours earlier at the dinner party. Washing a mouthful of delicious lasagna down with a sip of white wine, Michael had asked, a hint of trepidation in his voice, "By the way, have you guys read *The Dark Presence* yet?"

Mila had given Dennis that look. That rolling-eyed look. That picture that meant a thousand words. Then she'd said, "No, I haven't gotten around to it yet. Sorry, I can't even remember what I did with it."

To which Dennis had added: "I haven't had a chance to read it. I'm too busy right now." Turning to his not-so-lovely wife, he added: "I think you put it upstairs in your office, honey. On the bookshelves with all your other books."

"I just don't remember," she said.

"Or maybe you used it to line the kitty litter box," Dennis said, turning to Michael with a toothy grin, nudging his shoulder, and causing him to spill wine onto his steaming lasagna. "Just kidding."

Michael had almost choked on his lasagna.

Removing his winter jacket and hanging it in the closet, he tried to erase it from his mind, pacing around his large empty house, trying to work through the sadness and disappointment. The bitter rejection. *Exercise always cheers you up, right?* Not this time. Michael's mind kept returning to the dinner party rejection. The dinner party debacle. He plopped himself down in a chair at the kitchen table.

"Not any fucking more," he said. "I'm not hanging around with those fuckers anymore. Fuck their dinner parties. Fuck their fake support. Fuck their fake friendship. Fuck them!"

Michael sighed deeply, the litany of expletives going some way to making him feel better. Trying to cheer himself up, he went through a mental checklist of friends and family who *had* supported him in his writing endeavors.

Out of six immediate family members, including his mother and father, three had actually read and enjoyed his novels. And, although none of them had posted reviews—the elixir of life that authors rely on to survive and thrive in the industry—they'd all offered words of encouragement.

He counted up his friends. Good friends, not fake friends. He covered ten digits. *Not bad. Most people are lucky to count their good friends on one hand.*

He then went down the list of those who'd read some of his novels and those who hadn't.

Five of them had. Four had posted favorable reviews. After reading a horror novel, one friend, Dianne, had said, "I'm sorry, the book was well written, but it's just not my genre. I can't handle all that blood, guts, and gore. I was so disturbed and scared after reading it, I couldn't sleep for two nights."

Michael thought about it. Little did Dianne realize, she'd paid him the highest compliment he'd ever received. He was a horror writer after all. Sure, he was on a mission to educate, influence, and entertain. But, he was also on a mission to scare the hell out of his readers, at least the ones who liked having the hell scared out of them. It was nice to know he'd accomplished that with at least one reader.

And he'd made a point of thanking Dianne for reading *On Death's Doorstep*, explaining to her that true horror fans get a thrill out of being scared. He'd also apologized to her, and advised her not to read any more of his novels—if indeed she found them too disturbing. That was not his intention as a writer. To fuck up his reader's health.

Michael absently flicked on the TV, a small smile beginning to purse his lips. His reflections *were* beginning to cheer him up. And really, should he expect all of his close friends and family to take an interest in his writing? That was unrealistic at best, downright stupid at worst. Actually, he'd received more support, more positive feedback, more free promotion, and more five-star reviews from people he'd never met, legitimate book buyers who really enjoyed his novels.

Everyone has their own lives, their own problems, and their own shit. It was foolish to think that all of them would take an interest and encourage him in his work. He thought of something he'd read on people's ability to even listen to others, never mind having the capacity to encourage, read, and support them in their work.

It went something like this: We listen to half of what's being said. We give a shit about half of that. We understand half of that. We believe half of that, and we remember half of that. Now, what was it you were saying?

Michael watched five minutes of news and then turned the TV off. A seed of doubt was growing in his mind. He needed to chop it down before it festered into an infectious weed of hate and negativity.

Fake friends. If they don't give a shit about my passion in life, do they really give a shit about me? Probably not. Maybe I'll just cross them off my fucking friend list then. Chop off a few digits maybe.

***

Michael swam his way into consciousness from a nightmare-filled and fitful sleep early the next morning. He was still troubled by the dinner party debacle. He'd dreamt of visiting many homes as a spectral entity, a ghost who could walk through walls, watch and listen to conversations, unseen and unheard. He'd visited the homes of his critics and had heard what they were saying behind his back.

None of it was good.

"He's probably a hack. Not that I've read anything, so maybe I shouldn't say. But, he probably should've kept his day job."

"I couldn't tell him to his face but I hated the novel."

"When God was giving out brains, Michael thought He said trains and he took the caboose."

The last stop on the hellish nightmare train was the home of Mila and Dennis. They were having dinner, discussing Michael and his work.

"I don't really care what he writes," Dennis said. "I'm just not that interested."

"I'm pretty sure I've lost the book anyway," Mila answered. "So I couldn't read it if I wanted to. Not that I'd want to anyway. I doubt Michael can write at all."

"Exactly," Dennis said, stuffing his face with potatoes. "We've got enough of our own shit to deal with without worrying about what someone else is doing."

"That's right, baby. But, to shut him up, maybe we should just say we read it and loved it."

"Can't do that. What if he asks about specifics?"

"True enough. Let's leave it then, and hope he doesn't mention it again."

"I don't think he will. He only brought it up once in three months. Did you see the look on his face when I said we used his novel to line the kitty litter box?"

Uproarious laughter.

Michael frowned as snippets of the nightmare played over and over in his mind like a chilling horror movie. He knew a phone conversation with his mentor and close friend, Stephanie Bower, would set him straight. An accomplished horror author in her own right, she was brilliant at helping him view things from the proper perspective. Maybe it was better to discuss it face-to-face with her. Over coffee.

***

Stephanie had listened intently while Michael told the story. He'd watched her small features darken and her blue eyes harden. As he spoke, her cheeks had turned from white to bright pink.

"You wanna know what I think?" she said, eyes narrowing. Her hand tightened around her cardboard coffee cup. She frowned, noticing her firm grip squeezing too hard, threatening to explode its hot contents. She loosened her grip.

"That's why I'm here," Michael said. He knew he didn't have to tell Stephanie not to sugar-coat it.

"If they don't care about your passion, it usually means they don't give a fuck about you," she said. "It's really easy to spot the ones who fully support and hold a true interest in what we do and easy to spot the fake bastards who wear a mask of bullshit."

"My sentiments exactly."

"I've had total strangers offer positive comments on my books and buy them because they wanted to. To get compliments and positive feedback from people I don't know has been far more rewarding than anything I'd expect to get from a friend anyway. Maybe a friend doesn't want to hurt your feelings so they don't tell you the truth. They could easily lie and say how great the book was when really they thought it was a piece of shit. So, I never ask friends anymore. Or family either. Not that any of my family has ever shown any interest in my writing. I'd rather a stranger read my works; that way I have a better chance of hearing the truth instead of a pile of sugar-coated bullshit!"

"Or worse," Michael said, his mood darkening. "They never find the time to read it or have no interest in doing so and make all kinds of excuses. Like they used it to line the kitty litter box."

Stephanie was aghast. "Is that what they said?"

"That's what Dennis said. And they both grinned. Holding back laughter, you ask me."

"The lies, excuses, and jokes people conjure up for why they haven't read your book is mind-blowing."

"What do you think I should do?"

"I don't know these people. Never met them, and from what you say, I don't want to. Are they close friends of the inner circle kind, or just garden-variety friends?"

"I don't see them a whole lot. I don't call them much. Once in a blue moon I see them at a dinner party, either at my place or theirs. These happen maybe once a month and they're planned well in advance. You know me, I hate making plans. I'm more spontaneous. They're not the kind of friends I could call if I really had a problem; I mean they wouldn't give me the shirt off their back if I was desperate."

"More like acquaintances or casual friends then?"

"Fake friends."

"That's more like it," Stephanie said. "I think you should distance yourself from them. You have to ask yourself, do they really add anything positive to your life?"

"It's not all black and white, but for the most part no."

"It's never black and white. I have friends who just don't read for that matter. It would be stupid to ask them to support me or read one of my books. I have others that've told me it's not their genre, so fair enough. Still others feign interest, but I don't always blow them off. I have one friend who is going through so much emotional turmoil right now I don't think she's capable of bringing herself to a calm place where she can actually see outside of her own messed up bubble."

"That's true," Michael said, feeling encouraged. "I have family members who said they would read my books but never have. But otherwise, they're pretty good people. I don't take it personally, nor do I blow them off. I just recognize I'm not gonna get the kind of support I want from them and move on.

"Same here. As I said, I don't ask family or friends anymore. You can choose your friends but you can't choose your family. In your case, though, you're dealing with fake friends, as you say. Not even paying lip service to the notion of supporting you and probably even criticizing you behind your back. There is no mask of deceit there, it's all out there festering in the open from what you tell me."

Michael's nightmare flashed through his mind. He felt downright depressed all over again.

And evidently, Stephanie could read him like an open book. "Don't worry about it, Mike. I've read your books. I know you're a good writer. Not to mention all the people who've praised your work over the years that you don't even know."

"I guess you're right. But it still hurts."

"Don't worry," Stephanie said with a grin. "Karma's a bastard. One day maybe they'll both get torn a new asshole."

Michael admired that about Stephanie. She didn't mince words.

***

Mila looked at Dennis with concern. "Did you hear that?"

He washed down a mouthful of bread with a gulp of wine. "You mean the wind whistling? Yeah, I heard that. There's a storm coming, honey. Remember?"

Mila's eyes narrowed. "I know there's a storm coming, silly. We watched the news together. *Remember?* I'm not talking about the whipping wind. I heard a crashing sound outside in the backyard."

Dennis stood. "Probably the wind knocked down a garbage can or something. I'll go check."

Dennis went to the back door, put his boots and winter jacket on, and went outside. As soon as he stepped onto the back porch, a strong gust of wind slammed him into the door, blowing off his Budweiser cap and sweeping it into the neighbor's backyard. He watched it twirl in the air and disappear in the heavy snow. *Fucking white-out. Gonna be a nasty one.*

"Fucking bastard," he said, gripping the door handle with both hands and steadying himself. Ferocious winds and driving snow pounded him for a few seconds. Finally the wind let up and he scrambled down the stairs, trudged through a foot of snow, and arrived at the detached garage. The garbage cans were in the alley on the vehicle entrance side of the garage so he had to go into the building and press the automatic garage door opener before he would be able to see if the trash containers had been blown down the alley or not.

He opened the door quickly and slammed it shut behind him, a second after another strong gust of wind plastered the garage with a fresh carpet of snow. He flicked the light on and pressed the door opener. More lights came on and the garage door whirred to life and began rising. When it reached the top, he approached the vehicle entrance and looked outside. Three trash cans were halfway down the alley and garbage was strewn all over the white snow, assorted wind-whipped pieces spiraling around in the air like mini-tornadoes.

"Fuck me," he said, balling his fists. He was tempted to forget about the garbage cans, return to the house, and tell Mila he'd cleaned everything up. Of course, come morning he'd then have to explain three missing garbage cans. And he knew. Hell hath no fury like the wrath of Mila.

So he trudged down the alley, managed to retrieve two garbage cans, and began making his way back to the garage.

When he arrived, he placed one inside, rolling it to the front of the garage. He lifted the second one high over his head, hoping to set it on the workbench. But as he was putting it down, a strong gust of wind caught it and slammed it into the back of his head, catapulting him forward violently. He released the can, watching it teeter and roll and collide with the front fender of Mila's new SUV. He heard a metallic crunch.

At the same time, he fell forward, slamming his head on the corner of the workbench. As a dizzying constellation of stars danced around his head, he fell on his back on the concrete floor.

A gust of wind covered him with a blanket of snow as his head slowly began to clear. After unleashing a litany of profanity, he got up slowly, deciding wisely to forget about the other can. "And the fucking garbage."

He stumbled to the door, pressed the automatic garage door opener, and let out a deep sigh as he watched it wind down mechanically and clunk to a stop on the concrete floor. He rubbed a growing goose egg on the back of his head and felt fresh warm blood. He brought his other hand to a spot above his right eyebrow, and grimaced and as he felt another rising bump. At least there was no blood on that injury.

"What the hell happened to you?" his wife said as he staggered into the kitchen.

Dennis went over to the sink and stuck his bleeding head inside. "Help me, honey. I got attacked by a garbage can. Got attacked by my workbench. Got assaulted by the fucking snow and wind."

Mila rose quickly, fetching a clean towel and wiping the back of his blood-soaked head. Ten minutes later, she had him cleaned up, bandaged, and sitting comfortably, albeit dizzily, on the living room couch.

He'd explained most of the story to her. Then, through a slowly clearing fog, he noticed her right index finger was bandaged. "What happened to you?"

"Oh shit, just bad luck. While you were outside, I cut my finger with the butcher knife while I was trimming the roast."

"Are you okay?"

Mila nodded. "It was bleeding like crazy but it'll heal. What about you? Do you want me to take you to the hospital?"

Raw fear wrinkled Dennis's brow. "What, in this? Are you kidding? I'm okay. Just a minor concussion I think."

"We'll see how you feel tomorrow then."

"Okay."

"Did you recover all the garbage cans?"

"No. One got away."

"That's okay."

"And one more thing."

"What's that?"

"Your SUV?"

Mila's face tightened. "What about it?"

"I think there's a pretty nasty dent in the front fender. One of the garbage cans got away from me.

Mila's brow crinkled and she didn't say anything for a full minute. When she did open her mouth, Dennis was sure he'd be getting a tongue-lashing.

But all she said was, "I think I'm gonna turn in for the night. You'd be wise to do the same."

When they were all tucked into their queen-sized bed, Dennis cautiously put his hand on Mila's stomach. She tensed initially and he almost withdrew it. Then she relaxed and he left it there.

"Sorry about your SUV," Dennis said softly, his voice punctuated by windblown snow slamming the bedroom window.

"Don't worry about it," Mila said after a brief pause.

"Why do you think we're getting so much bad luck lately?"

"I wish I knew, Dennis. I wish I knew."

***

Michael hung up his coat in the hallway closet and put his snow-covered boots in a rubber boot tray inside the closet. He'd driven home white-knuckled after dining by himself in a nearby Chinese restaurant. Visibility had been reduced to almost zero as a result of the blizzard and he'd narrowly avoided a four-vehicle collision. *It's only gonna get worse. Wouldn't be surprised if I lose power.*

He lived by himself in a five-bedroom bungalow on a cul-de-sac in an upper-middle class neighborhood. After making a hot herbal tea, he went into his main-floor office, knocked off 563 words on his latest novel, and decided to go to bed.

Curled up in bed a few minutes later and listening to his 1959-built home creak and groan with the force of the storm, Michael felt strangely vindicated. He didn't understand why, nor did he wish to analyze the feeling for fear of stirring up more mentally deleterious memories of the dinner party debacle. *Probably just Stephanie's pep talk. Leave it at that.*

Fifteen minutes later he fell fast asleep.

In the dark of night, lit faintly by numerous dots shimmering below him, Michael wiped blinding snow from his eyes and strode effortlessly down a city street. He was a giant on an evening stroll in suburban Calgary. But it was more than a stroll. It was a mission. And he didn't question whether his mission was real or fake, only knew it had to be done. He found the house, knelt down on one knee, and peered into the window. He saw them sleeping not-so-peacefully, tossing and turning under the glow of a purple nightlight. He tapped on the window with his knuckle and it shattered, blowing snow and glass into the bedroom.

Mila leaped from the bed, grabbing a housecoat and throwing it over her slim body. Her eyes were wide with terror. Her tongue hung from her mouth like a rabid dog. "You. What do you want?"

Dennis lifted his head from the pillow, screamed, and fainted.

"Karma's a bastard," Michael said with a satisfied grin. "It tears you a new asshole when you least expect it."

"No, no," Mila said in a high-pitched voice. "I'll read your goddamned stupid book if that's what you want."

"Too little too late," Michael said. "You had your chance."

He reached over and grabbed a power pole with a streetlight mounted on top. With a rubber-gloved hand, he tore it from its concrete foundation, snapping it like a twig, and smashing it through Mila and Dennis's bedroom window. As the power pole sizzled and crackled with electrical sparks, he stood up, wiped his hands, and grinned, pleased with his handy work.

"That should do it," Michael said, as the house burst into flames.

As he floated away, he could hear the horrifying screams of Mila and Dennis as their home snapped, crackled, and popped.

It was music to his ears.

***

It took him more than two hours the next morning to shake off the powerful feeling of dread. The nightmare felt so real, unlike anything he'd ever experienced before. When he'd finally calmed down and convinced himself it was nothing more than a bad dream, he showered, dressed, and peered out his front window.

At least three feet of snow. And the blizzard was still raging. Fortunately, it hadn't killed his power last night. Michael went into the kitchen, poured himself a cup of coffee, went into the living room, and plopped himself down on the sofa. He flicked on the TV and quickly surfed over to a local news station. He was anxious to see what kind of devastation the storm had caused and still was causing.

A clean-cut male anchor sat in a news studio reporting on several school closures, adding that all federal government offices would be closed for the day due to the severe blizzard. He went on to report three storm-related traffic accidents, one of which had resulted in two fatalities.

Then the blue-suited anchor picked up a piece of paper from his desk and his spectacle-framed eyes widened, magnified comically by thick lenses.

He cleared his throat. "This just in. Last night the storm knocked down a power pole in the suburban district of Somerset, smashing it through a home occupied by Dennis and Mila Steinweister."

Michel froze, spilling hot coffee.

"Fire fighters and paramedics rushed to the scene but..."

BOOM!

The TV died. The lights went out.

Michael suddenly heard another loud *BOOM* and saw sparks fly from a nearby power pole. He rushed to his bay window and watched in terror as a large transformer explosion sent electrical wires flying everywhere. The wires sizzled across the snow—cracking, snapping, and writhing like poisonous snakes before fizzling out and growing still.

His body convulsing with fear, he paced the floor frantically, trying unsuccessfully to convince himself that he had nothing to do with Mila and Dennis's...death? *But are they dead? And if they are, how could I have done it? How could it be me? I was home sleeping.*

His eyes strayed to the small foyer at his front door. On the tiled floor stood his water-soaked winter boots. Beside them, his crumpled winter jacket.

A rush of fear-fueled adrenaline shot through his body and he convulsed as if struck by a bolt of lightning.

In the rush of emotions that followed, he didn't know what was real, what was fake; what was true, what was false.

However, it didn't take him long to realize that one thing was true. Arriving home last night, he was positive he'd hung up his coat in the hallway closet and set his snow-covered boots in a rubber boot tray inside the closet.

Oh my God! Did I kill them?

An hour later, he still didn't have any answers. He was more confused and distraught than ever. To try and make sense of the nerve-rattling experience, he went into his office and powered up his laptop. He planned on using what battery life that remained to document the ordeal. At the very least it would be therapeutic.

At the very best, it would make a damn fine horror tale.

The title came to him in an instant.

Fake Friends.

The Stalker

Admiring the crimson setting sun on his gorgeous beachfront, Ronnie Garber was thrilled. And he had every reason to be. He'd finally done it. Escaped the rat race. Jumped off that never-ending treadmill of capitalism. No longer competing with his colleagues, buying stupid toys, doing stupid renovations to his city home, not because he needed or wanted them. Just because he'd wanted to one-up his colleagues at the accounting firm. It had been a futile and fruitless waste of time. But those days were long gone. He was a city bean-counter-turned-country-bumpkin. At 46, he'd retired early from the firm, bought his dream acreage homestead on Prince Edward Island, and gotten the hell out of the crazy and stressful city of Toronto. One week ago, he'd arrived at the airport, met his realtor, rented a car, and followed him to his dream home.

He'd spent the last few weeks clearing the road to the beach, painting, decorating, and furnishing the modest turn-of-the-century two-story home. Getting it ready for the arrival of his friends, Brad and Cindy, Amanda and Caleb. They'd be arriving tomorrow evening and he had everything just about done. A few stops tomorrow. Booze run. A few more groceries. Some plastic lawn chairs for the new oceanfront fire pit, and voila, everything would be picture-perfect for the arrival of his houseguests.

In other circles, he might feel like a fifth wheel, the odd man out, but not with these folks. It didn't matter to them that he was still single. They were close, inner-circle friends and they loved him for who he was, not for who he was with.

He was sure he'd be able to find the woman of his dreams here and when time permitted would meet the neighbors and try to involve himself in community activities. But he wasn't in any hurry. That could wait until that euphoric pinch-me-I'm-dreaming feeling started to wear off.

He sighed, watching the last remnants of a spectacular sunset disappear on the horizon.

Crack... snap...

He spun around, shining his flashlight at the bushes from where the sounds had originated. His heart beat faster and in icicle of cold fear pricked the nape of his neck. He shuddered. *Just a wild animal. You're in the forest now, buckaroo.*

But, despite his self-assurances, he said, "Anyone there?"

Nothing.

Summoning some courage, he moved stealthily toward the trees. The sounds appeared to have come from a distance of about fifty feet. *Snap...crack.* His own feet crunching twigs startled him a second time, and he stopped.

"I said is there anyone there?"

He thought he saw a small white light. Was it only a firefly in July? He heard more rustling and then what sounded like footfalls, retreating at a rapid pace. He stood stock-still listening to the sounds fade away and then disappear. *Probably a coyote. Maybe a fox. Maybe a raccoon. Nothing to worry about, that's for sure.*

After a few minutes of inner dialogue, he'd gone a long way to convincing himself it was just a wild animal. As he climbed into his pickup, a feeling of excitement settled in. *This is gonna be fun.* At least for the time being, he'd buried the shadow of doubt deep into a small compartment of his mind, locked the door, and thrown away the key.

***

"Wow, this property is gorgeous," Caleb said, already beginning to slur his words less than two hours after he'd arrived.

"Thanks," Ronnie said. "I love it."

Caleb leaned over, reached into the cooler, and grabbed another beer. "Want one?"

"Sure."

Caleb tossed it over and Ronnie caught it and cracked it.

"Anyone else?" Caleb asked.

The others declined. None of them were drinking as fast as Caleb, except maybe Ronnie.

Ronnie and his friends sat around a campfire in a tree-lined clearing about fifty feet from the water's edge. The small burned brightly, sending hot embers popping into the clear night sky. The moon was almost full. A million stars blinked and twinkled in the sky. The temperature was a balmy 24 degrees Celsius. The sound of gently lapping waves swished on the nearby shoreline. A postcard-perfect night.

"You really lucked out buying this place," Amanda said. "Me and Caleb have to plant trees where we live and you've gotta cut them down. I'm jealous."

"It's a beautiful forest," Ronnie agreed. "Mother Nature at her ever-lovin' finest."

"You got that right," Brad said, touching Cindy's arm gently. "What do you think, hon?"

"It's paradise," Cindy said. "I'm jealous too. All of us still stuck in the rat-race chasing a fucking fictitious materialistic dream and you had the common sense to cut your losses and get the fuck out."

"I don't think I cut any losses," Ronnie said. "I've dropped my living expenses down to a third of what I was paying in Toronto. And here I have way more to show for it. What did I lose? Well, I did leave a bunch of good friends behind to come here, you guys especially, but, hey, you're here now, visiting. And I can visit you, not that I'd want to hit the rat-race again any time soon. No offense."

"None taken," Cindy said. "I didn't really mean cut your losses. You know what I meant. You've simplified your life. To do that you had to make sacrifices. I'd love it here myself. But I've got a partner." She leaned over and kissed Brad on the cheek.

"I haven't had a chance to explore the social scene here," Ronnie said, rubbing his three-day chin stubble. He grinned, knowing he couldn't have gotten away with any chin-scratch as an accountant in a big city. "But, I hope I can meet someone here. You know, get some friends. Maybe a girlfriend. All in good time. I'm still waiting for this dream-like buzz to wear off before I start exploring those waters."

"Have you met any of your neighbors yet?" Brad asked, reaching out and stroking Cindy's hand. She smiled and clasped his hand tightly in hers.

"Met the guy across the highway from me. Paul Pebble. They call him Happy Rock."

A few chuckles.

Ronnie continued: "He doesn't seem all that sociable but I get the sense I can trust him and he already said he'd be willing to help me out if I needed anything. I've already borrowed his wheelbarrow and bought some used furniture from him. He helped me carry it in and everything."

"I hear Islanders are the salt of the earth," Cindy said. "Very friendly, trustworthy, and loyal people."

"I've heard the same thing," Ronnie said. "And I'm sure for the most part that's true. Time will tell, I suppose. Time will tell. But I'm looking forward to my new adventure."

Craaaaaaack!

A split-second of silence followed by audible gasps from Amanda and Brad.

"What the fuck was that?" Caleb said, leaping from his chair. He was a lieutenant in the infantry division of the Canadian military, had done several Afghanistan tours, and was strung tighter than a guitar; shell-shocked from his harrowing combat experiences. His hand quickly went to his waist, clicking open a leather knife sheath, and pulling out a military-issue combat knife. He moved a few feet toward the source of the noise and shone his flashlight into the trees.

Ronnie hadn't mentioned anything to the group about last night's fright. He'd mostly forgotten about it. "Hey, easy, bro. It's probably just a wild animal."

"Shit, that scared me," Brad said, also standing up.

"Who the fuck is in there?" Caleb asked, moving into the forest.

It all happened so fast. The others just watched him go.

"Be careful," Ronnie said. "Lots of trip hazards out here." Although he doubted Caleb would have any trouble. Fit and muscular, clean-cut, and combat-ready, he was often mistaken for a cop.

A few seconds later, from deep within the woods, they heard laughter, followed by the fading sound of twigs snapping.

Caleb emerged from the forest. "Raccoon, folks," he said. "Only a raccoon. Carry on drinking."

And that they did. Someone produced a battery-operated transistor radio, hung it on a tree branch and soon they were having the time of their lives. Everyone was getting a little, if not a lot, tipsy. Caleb set up a flashlight on a log table and beamed it into the tree line. When someone stood in front of it, it created elongated, shadowy body doubles as tall as fifty-foot spruce trees. Cindy and Brad, Amanda and Caleb, gyrated to CCR's Bad Moon Rising, their gigantic black shadows in perfect synchronicity with their dance moves.

Ronnie sat in a plastic lawn chair pounding back beers and laughing hysterically. "Hey, we've got a party of eight. I love it. Keep going guys."

"You forgot about Ronnie," Amanda said. She motioned to him with a wave of her hand, spilling some of her vodka cooler.

"Get up here," Amanda called to Ronnie. "You've got a partner. A black shadow man."

Ronnie got up, cracked another beer from the cooler, and began gyrating to the music. At one point he twirled close enough to a large pine tree and made a hugging motion, grinning as his black shadow man partner hugged the tree and caressed it lovingly.

It brought the group to uproarious laughter.

Brad, unwilling to be outdone, sashayed over to a tree and laughed hysterically as his black shadow double began humping it spasmodically.

Ronnie pointed, struggling to contain a laugh. "Look, a tree fucker."

More out-of-control laughter.

***

Disgusting, Esmerelda Bakersfield thought as she entered her house. *Disrespecting Mother Nature like that is disgusting.* But she had more important things on her mind right now. Her head was aching, the voices were starting to rumble, and, hiking home through the dark forest, she'd started once again to see all manner of demons that haunted her regularly; horned devils with serpent-like tongues; giant, venom-spitting, slithery snakes. But what had terrorized her the most was the Shadow People and the horrifying Hat Man. Summoned, she believed, by that new guy next door, just beyond that three hundred foot tree bluff that separated the properties.

"No... no... no," she said, entering her bathroom, opening the medicine cabinet with an unsteady hand, and reaching for a pill jar. Nervously, she shook two loose, tossed them in her mouth, and washed them down with a glass of water. She wiped her wrinkled chin, ran a hand through her long grey-blonde hair, and quickly grabbed two more pill bottles. She opened one, chased down two more pills with water, and repeated the procedure with the other pill jar. She then grabbed a towel, wiped water dribble from her cheek, and caught a glance of her reflection in the mirror.

Blue eyes, bug eyes. Her pupils were dilated. Her mouth hung open as if a horrific scream was trying to force itself into existence. Her brow was crinkled beyond repair. She felt her stomach lurch, pulled down her pants, farted loudly and pungently, and a liquid bowel movement gushed out, splashing into the water and toilet bowl just as she sat down.

No doubt about it. She was scared shitless.

Esmerelda was a rare and sorrowful breed. She suffered from manic depression, paranoid schizophrenia, and obsessive-compulsive disorder, all tightly wrapped into one neat little gift. She was on a regiment of drugs, a pharmaceutical cocktail prescribed to control her numerous mental maladies. Her condition was exacerbated by the fact that her parents, who had tragically and mysteriously died ten years ago while hiking through the forest at night, had left her alone in the world. She'd inherited the family home. She'd lived in that old house alone for the last ten years—isolated, friendless, and arguably bat-shit crazy.

A little later, the pills had gone some way to washing away the demons. She sat on her couch sipping herbal tea, trying to calm her nerves and think her way out of this latest and tragic development.

A new neighbor had moved in next door. She'd seen enough to know. He was an evil new neighbor. He and his friends didn't understand what they were doing. Maybe they did. Maybe they wanted to taunt, tease, and terrorize her. Whatever the reason, they were willingly and carelessly conducting satanic rituals and invoking the horrifying Shadow People and the terrifying Hat Man, both spectral entities that had haunted her for as long as she could remember.

Her head was somewhat clear now. The voices had slowed to a dull roar, a mildly intrusive whisper. The hallucinations had disappeared. Jesus, her one and only savior, had scattered the monsters. Brushed them away with his almighty hand. But for how long? She must do something about this new neighbor. Must do it now before he unleashes the unspeakable evil the Hat man is capable of.

As the minutes ticked away, a plan started to jell in Esmerelda's unstable mind. A comfortable buzz began to settle over her as the chemical cocktail kicked into overdrive. A few of the wrinkles on her brow flattened out. Her pupils returned to normal. Her heart rate slowed. A malicious grin began to dance across her tight lips.

I know just what to do. Meet fire with fire.

***

"I heard you last night."

The tone was contemptuous. The voice was high-pitched and almost shrill. Ronnie just about jumped out of his skin when he heard it. He was pounding nails, repairing some loose boards on his back porch, probably not the best task given all the beers he'd pounded back last night.

Despite their indulgences, his friends had gotten up early and gone off sightseeing and shopping.

He spun around quickly, almost dropping the hammer. A large woman, early sixties maybe, stood a short distance behind him. Her arms were crossed over her humongous breasts and a look of consternation—or maybe constipation—tightened her thin lips. She wore a white, food-stained floral apron over a long and flowing red summer dress. Her hair was in disarray.

"Jesus Christ," Ronnie said, his head still aching dully from last night's festivities. "You scared the hell out of me."

Esmerelda frowned. "You shouldn't use the Lord's name in vain."

Ronnie wasn't exactly in the mood for apologies, given the way she'd crept up on him and trespassed on his property. "Who are you?" He almost added, "And what the fuck are you doing here?" but bit his tongue.

"I'm Esmerelda. You're neighbor next door. I heard you last night."

In spite of his rising agitation, Ronnie put the hammer down—a more useful function for the hammer occurred to him as he did—and offered his hand. "Ronnie."

She shook it, but only for a millisecond.

Her hand felt like a cold, wet dishrag.

She wiped her hand on her apron, narrowing her eyes and examining it like it was infected.

"Sorry, did we keep you up last night?" Ronnie asked.

Since the beach was almost a mile from his house, yet still very much on his property, Ronnie had difficulty believing, in the cover of the sound-dampening and thick forest, that she could have heard the revelry or the small transistor radio. But he gave her the benefit of the doubt. He didn't want enemies, especially with his neighbors.

"A little bit," Esmerelda said. "But I left after you summoned the Shadow People and the Hat Man."

Looney tunes, Ronnie thought. He didn't know anything about the Shadow People or the Hat Man. Or was she referring to the shadow dancing? But, wouldn't that mean she'd done more than heard them?

"You saw us?" he asked.

"I watched you from the forest," she said matter-of-factly.

The comment hit Ronnie upside the head like a sucker punch. "You watched us from the forest?" Ronnie didn't know what else to say. That clearly meant she'd trespassed. Clearly meant she'd been stalking them late at night. What had he gotten himself into?

"I often wander through the forest," she said. "You don't own the beach, you know."

Ronnie knew the law governing Canadian oceanfront properties. The land below the high tide mark, which typically represents much of the sandy beach, is owned by the provincial government and therefore technically public property. Anyone can walk along or sit at the shoreline, providing they don't cross through private property without permission to do it. When he'd first purchased his property, Ronnie had studied the land surrounding the house next door. His neighbor's house. No waterfront property. Which meant she would have had to be wandering through his forest. Hell, she'd just admitted as much. *Don't push it, buddy. Keep the peace, remember.*

"I know that," Ronnie said. "Did you take one of the trails on my property to reach us?"

"No," Esmerelda said. "The trail starts on my property but intersects with yours a half-mile or so from the water's edge. I just walked the rest of the way down the new road you cleared."

Ronnie was about to say something nasty but bit his tongue a second time. Maybe that's just what they did around here. Walk all over everyone else's property and call it their own. Maybe it was one big happy family. *But the stalking. I don't call that one big happy family. I call that pretty fucked up.*

It was as if Esmerelda could read his mind. "In case you're wondering, my grandfather used to own your house. At that time we had trails all over the place going from my property to yours. Nobody cared."

Ronnie was momentarily at a loss for words. He didn't want to discourage her from using the beach, even if it meant crossing his property to do it. On the other hand, he sure as hell didn't want her stalking him in the middle of the night, or sneaking up behind him and taking him by surprise as she'd just done. Then, as if by divine intervention, an idea occurred to him.

"One big happy family I suppose," Ronne finally said.

Esmerelda just nodded as a hint of sadness passed through her blue eyes.

Suddenly Ronnie felt bad for saying it. But it didn't stop him. "Well, I'd be careful, trekking through the forest late at night alone. It could be dangerous."

Esmerelda backed away a few steps. "What do you mean?"

"We heard a pack of coyotes howling last night. You know that frenzied sound they make when they've circled their kill; they all start howling to distract it, and then they move in for the kill en masse and tear it to shreds?"

Two more steps back. Eyes widening. "There are no coyotes at the beach there."

But Ronnie knew he had her. He could see the fear in her eyes. And, they had heard coyotes howling at the moon last night, a few minutes before they'd all turned in. It hadn't bothered any of them. They'd joked about it, and even enjoyed the mysterious and spooky sounds.

"There was a pack of them really close to us last night," Ronnie said. "So, I'd be careful if I were you. You never know what they'd do to a lone female if they were hungry enough."

"I... I better go," Esmerelda said, a blush beginning to creep across her otherwise pallid complexion.

Ronnie watched silently as she spun around and began marching away purposefully. He waited until she had progressed a good thirty feet or so before saying, "By the way..."

She stopped and turned around.

He continued: "If you hear some noise later this afternoon, it's just me with the chainsaw. Mr. Stihl and I are gonna be knocking down some standing-dead trees next to my new road. Widow makers... I think that's what you guys call them. But, don't worry, we won't be cutting late at night. We won't keep you up."

Clenching her fists, Esmerelda stared at him for a long moment, spun around, and left without saying another word.

Ronnie watched her slip down a small path and disappear into the woods. He found himself second-guessing his decision to leap off the capitalist treadmill. *This could be a problem. This could really be a problem.*

***

By 4:36 that afternoon, Ronnie had the chainsaw out halfway down his beach road. He'd texted Caleb, telling him where they could find him, even though he knew, given how quiet it was here, they'd be able to hear him in a heartbeat as soon as they returned. But Caleb had indicated a willingness to help him knock down widow makers, so he'd wanted to keep them apprised of his endeavors.

He'd already cut down some small diseased birch trees overhanging the road, trees that would inevitably get knocked down in winter storms and block the road, or worse, land on him or his pickup. He sized up a dead spruce tree. About eight inches thick and a good forty feet tall. It was tilted at an odd angle, leaning toward some other tall and healthy trees. He knew if he cut it where it was leaning it would very likely get snagged in the healthy trees and then he'd have to fasten a chain to the pickup tow hitch and pull it down. If possible, he wanted to avoid that. Although he'd learned to use a chainsaw as a young boy during visits to his grandfather's farm in northern Ontario, he fully understood the dangers of logging alone. One miscalculation and it could be lights out. Permanently. A game of inches. But that didn't really scare him. He enjoyed the adrenaline rush of man versus nature. Actually, the way he viewed it was man in harmony with nature. Cutting down dead trees would make room for more healthy ones to grow. Managing a renewable resource. Forest Management 101.

He removed his baseball cap, wiped a sweaty brow, ran a hand through his thick brown hair, and studied the tree. He sized up a three-foot opening between trees and decided to angle it that way. He fired up Mister Stihl, whom he revered as a deity of sorts. Mister Stihl had gotten him out of more binds than he cared to remember. As the chainsaw roared to life, he felt a surge of adrenaline. "Okay, brother, we got this."

He moved over to the tree, bent down, and notched one side, careful to angle it slightly away from its obvious trajectory.

He went behind the notch and started angling the back cut, tilting it downward slightly, knowing that once it hit the notch, the hinge would take over, guiding it to the ground. Even though he'd cut down hundreds of trees, it always made him a little nervous and very appreciative of the precariousness and preciousness of life.

He reached a certain point and heard a loud *crack*. He removed the chainsaw, stood back, and waited. The tree started slowly tilting toward the other trees. He shut down Mister Stihl and set him down. He stepped forward, leaned into the tree, and pushed, changing its trajectory just enough. It angled left, crashed into healthy tree branches, caught for a second, and then rolled down the branches, snapping one off, and smashing into the forest floor with a loud thud.

Ronnie sighed, unable to contain the feeling of giddiness enveloping him. He cracked his water bottle, guzzling four large gulps. "Yeah!"

He knew his angles were slightly off. Other than the token effort he'd put forth helping the loggers remove overgrowth on the beach road before the bush hog had cut a swath to the beach, it had been years since he'd picked up a chainsaw. But he also realized that, over time, his chainsaw skills would return. It was like riding a bike. You never forget.

He bent down to retrieve the chainsaw. Now it was time to buck the timber, stock the beach site with some, and put a few logs in his barn for the winter. Fortunately, his home had come equipped with a wood stove. And he had plenty of fuel—way, way more than he would ever burn in a lifetime.

"Nice work!"

Caleb, dressed in steel-toed boots and wearing protective eye-glasses and heavy-duty work gloves, moved toward him. He carried a small six-pack cooler. Ronnie doubted he ever left home without it.

"Hey, bro," Ronnie said. "Thanks. I'm still a little rusty, but it'll come back."

Caleb eyed the trajectory. "You didn't snag it in the other trees."

"A little bit. But it dropped."

Caleb reached into his cooler, pulled out a Budweiser can, and offered it to Ronnie.

"Beer and chainsaws mix?"

Caleb pushed the beer in his face playfully. "Come on. One won't kill you."

"Okay, okay." Ronnie took the beer, cracked it, and took a long pull. "That does taste good. Maybe beer and chainsaws mix quite well."

Caleb cracked a beer, sipped, and grinned. "We're gonna find out."

Caleb told Ronnie about what they'd done that day. A scenic coastal drive; a sightseeing stop at Panmure Island beach; lunch at the Tailgate Pub; grocery shopping, and booze refueling. "The others are taking a nap. Bunch of wimps."

Ronnie was about to tell Caleb about Esmerelda but was torn. But his friends only had two weeks here. And they'd been raving about his paradise and he didn't want to rain on their paradise parade. Yet if his neighbor presented a real threat and he said nothing, how would that work out? *It wouldn't work out.*

However, Caleb basically decided for him.

"As we drove in, I noticed your next-door neighbor at the end of her driveway. Just staring at us. I waved to her, but she didn't wave back. Maybe she didn't see me because the girls wanted the air-conditioning on so we had the windows closed. Either way, I didn't get a good feeling. Kind of creepy. Have you met her yet?"

"This afternoon. She came up behind me while I was repairing some boards on the porch and scared the shit out of me."

"What?"

A feeling of gloom settled over Ronnie as he relayed the rattling rendezvous with Esmerelda. He told Caleb everything.

"Holy shit," Caleb said. "I thought that was more than a raccoon last night. Something in the back of my mind told me it was a threat."

"Your combat training."

"Exactly."

"What should we do? I don't wanna make enemies with my neighbors?"

"Maybe your coyote story worked. Let's forget about it for now and get some work done. I wanna get my ass stationary so I can pound back some more beers. I don't really give a fuck about that bitch. And she sure as hell ain't gonna ruin my vacation."

They set to work bucking all the trees that Ronnie had cut, piling the smaller branches off to the side of the road and marking them with blue marking tape for future clean-up burns. Caleb cut down one more standing-dead tree, Ronnie the other. Without incident. Perfect angles. Perfect drops. They collected one load of wood and stacked it in the barn and drove another load down to the beach fire pit site, stacking it neatly between two large spruce trees.

After a booze-laced, fun-filled BBQ at the house, they drove down to the beach site. For good measure, Ronnie brought along Mister Stihl.

By 8:36 pm, they had another respectable blaze going. Caleb had already filled the others in on the Esmerelda ordeal, preferring disclosure over cover-up; caution over carelessness. He was a soldier after all.

They sat comfortably, enjoying fireside drinks and fireside chat.

"What's with the chainsaw?" Amanda asked.

"Thought maybe I'd fire it up as a sort of deterrence," Ronnie said. "To keep you-know-who away."

"I think the coyote story will fuck her up," Caleb said.

"She looked rattled with that one," Ronnie said. "But I wanted some insurance."

The sun was just beginning to set over the forest, blanketing the sky with bright pinks and fiery reds. Enough light to see a little but not a lot.

Caleb began surveying the freshly cut perimeter. He stopped in front of a standing-dead maple tree, angled awkwardly toward the fire pit. Toward them.

"Hey, we're in the line of fire. Another widow maker. You guys must have missed it."

"It's tough to get them all the first time around," Ronnie said. "Others show their faces later."

"Should we cut it down?" Caleb asked. "Put it out of its misery?"

"What misery?" Brad said. "It's already dead. You're just talking about giving it a proper burial."

"How about a cremation?" Caleb said, heading toward the pickup truck where Mister Stihl sat battle-ready. The chainsaw seemed to be smiling. Or was it a contemptuous grin?

"You've already had too much to drink," Amanda said. "Don't, honey."

But Caleb had already picked up Mister Stihl and was heading toward the dead maple.

"I'll be careful," he said with a grin. "Besides, it'll scare the shit out of the stalker." He waved his arm. "Get out of the way, you guys. Ronnie, get over here. Shine a light for me."

Brad stood. "Put it down, Caleb. I've got the stalker covered." He cupped his hands over his mouth. "Ooooooooooohhh... ooooooooooooooooooeeeeww! There, does that sound like a coyote?"

"Pretty convincing," Cindy said.

"Sounds more like a dog in heat, you ask me," Caleb said. "Now, come on. Clear out."

Ronnie grabbed a flashlight and approached the widow maker. He knew Caleb well enough to know that, once he put his mind to something, there was no stopping him. Especially when he was drunk.

***

Esmerelda heard the roar of the engine—*Vroom... vrooooom... vrooooooom!*—and stopped, her flashlight hand beginning to twitch. Her mind was sufficiently lubed up with prescription drugs and she'd dismissed the coyote and chainsaw stories as nothing more than manufactured bullshit, although that wouldn't have been her phrase of choice.

The voices had gotten the better of her earlier and she had to leave the house. Had to go into the forest. Had to see what her new neighbor was up to. It was just something that had to be done.

But the engine had scared her senseless and she stood frozen to the spot, trying to analyze her way out of it. But before the roar of the engine. *Wasn't that the sound a coyote howling? Looks like a duck, walks like a duck, quacks like a duck. It's a duck. No. They're just messing with me. Trying to scare me.* She caught her breath, mustered some courage, and carried on.

She moved slowly, weaving between the trees, searching for the spot where her property ended and Ronnie's began. The point of no return. *If he thinks he owns the beach, he's got another think coming.* Hearing a loud crash, followed by screams of delight or screams of anguish, she couldn't discern, she froze.

In the balmy July heat, she suddenly felt cold. Her heart raced. Fearing she would hyperventilate, she started taking deep breaths. In spite of her efforts, her heart continued to race. And then she heard it again, much closer and much louder now.

Vroom... vrooooom... vroooooom!!

And it was—*no, please, God no*—racing through the forest right toward her. Panic seized her. She spun around slammed into a tree, landing on the forest carpet, her penlight squirting loose from her hand. She tried to scream but nothing would emerge. The chainsaw, Mr. Stihl, was taking her breath away. As a bolt of adrenaline shot through her body, she got to her knees and began fumbling around for the penlight.

Vroom... vrooooom... vroooooom!!!

Crawling around, flailing her arms helplessly, she skinned her knee on a large razor-sharp dead branch. She heard it tear through her cotton summer slacks, felt it grow claws, or maybe fangs, and then rake down her legs.

Sharp pain. Blood flowing freely.

"Oww... oww... oww... God, Jesus, somebody save me. Pleeeeeease!"

Vroom... vrooooom... vroooooooooooooooooooom!!!!

She saw a bead of light flickering below her elbow and reached for it. The penlight. She tried to sigh, but her breathing was still so constricted and so erratic. All that escaped was a slow moan. Scrambling to her feet, she rushed back toward her house, still hearing the chainsaw, three *vrooms*, two *vrooms*, one *vroom* behind her. She finally hit the clearing surrounding her house and broke into a run. Reaching her concrete porch, she tripped on a step, flew toward the door, and grabbed a metal railing at the last second, narrowly avoiding a head-on collision. She slammed the door behind her, ran upstairs, rushed down the hallway, entered her bedroom, slammed and locked the door behind her, and jumped into bed.

Panting for breath, she pulled the covers up over her head. And listened. Listened for the sounds of Mister Stihl and the sounds of Mr. Coyote. Faintly, a good distance away, she heard the unmistakable sound of his engine roar to life. Then there was silence. The only thing she heard was the sound of her rasping breath, struggling to find normalcy. Finally her heart rate slowed and after a few minutes, she began breathing evenly.

Approximating normal. But not quite there. Maybe, after this ordeal, never quite there.

She tried to reassure herself. *My imagination. Took too many pills. My mind playing tricks on me. Mr. Stihl, Mr. Coyote, weren't chasing me at all. Too many pills. Mind playing tricks on me.* As the sound of silence shrouded her senses, Esmerelda almost smiled.

Until:

Vroom... vrooooom... vroooooom!!

And then:

Ooooooooooohhh... ooooooooooooooooeeeeww!

She crammed her hands to her ears and screamed: "Aaaaaaaaaaaaaaaeeeeeeeeeeeeoooooooh!!!"

Even in her terror, she realized there were only two choices: Either she had taken leave of her senses.

Or, it was her time to die.

***

Ronnie struggled to move his leg. No use. It was stuck. Stuck under a tree. He guessed the beachfront logging effort hadn't gone that well. But, that was the weird thing. It seemed to him it had. Hadn't Caleb dropped the deceased tree perfectly, even aligning the top of it right over the fire pit? Cut as you burn, burn as you cut. What could be more perfect than that? But here he was, trapped under a fallen tree, struggling to get his leg free. He looked around in the darkness.

"Hey, where are you guys? Get me outta here." Silence. Not even the roar of Mister Stihl. Not even the howling of Mr. Coyote. What the hell had gone wrong? He began pushing on the log, grunting and groaning, huffing and puffing. But nothing. The eight-inch diameter tree wouldn't budge an inch. It hadn't occurred to him that his leg should be hurting, maybe even be covered in blood.

"Come on, guys. I'm not fucking around here. Help me!"

Still nothing. Becoming seized by panic, he struggled fruitlessly for a moment until he heard something in the distance. Was it a coyote? Was it a pack of coyotes coming to devour him? Was it Mister Stihl coming to decapitate him?

He strained to identify the sound, now growing nearer.

Wee-woo-wee-woo-weeeeeee-wooooooooo!

Wait a minute. That's a siren. Coming to rescue me.

He bolted up in bed, his heart pounding, drawing in rapid breaths. *Thank God. A dream. A nightmare.*

Wee-woo-wee-woo-weeeeeee-wooooooooo!

The siren. Still there. Still coming closer.

He dressed quickly and rushed outside. The sound drew nearer and then turned unmistakably into the driveway next to his. Esmerelda's house. He thought about running over there but quickly changed his mind. He didn't even know what was going on and didn't want to be accused of anything. Through a hungover and foggy mind, he tried to piece together the events of last night. Caleb had indeed dropped the standing-dead tree perfectly. They'd cut it into fire wood, stacking some pieces and burning others, and then put the chainsaw away at a decent hour. *Did we? Yes, we did.*

The sound of the siren died.

What happened to Esmerelda?

He went inside the house and checked the time. It was early. 7:36 am. The others were still sleeping. He splashed some cold water on his face, prepared a pot of coffee, poured himself one, went outside, and sat on the back porch.

He heard faint conversation coming from next door, heard another vehicle pull into the driveway, and listened intently to what he assumed was the mechanical sounds of a stretcher being wheeled into her house. A few minutes later, more conversation, doors slamming, and the sound of a vehicle exiting. He fought off the urge to investigate.

Then the siren again.

Wee-woo-wee-woo-weeeeeee-woooooooo!

After the sound of the siren had faded into the distance, a cop car pulled into his driveway and he almost spilled hot coffee on his t-shirt. He gasped as the clean-cut uniformed cop stopped the car, climbed out, and approached him.

Ronnie then stepped off the porch and approached the cop car.

The man met him halfway and extended a hand. "Sorry to bother you, sir. I'm Officer Lance Jenkins with the Montague RCMP detachment."

Ronnie extended a hand, shook it, and released it. *Firm grip.* "Ronnie Garber."

"It's probably nothing, but I do have to follow this up."

"What happened?"

"Do you live here?"

"Yeah, just moved in."

"Not from around these parts?"

"No. Calgary."

"Right. Your neighbor, Esmerelda, had a bit of a nervous breakdown. She's going in for a psych evaluation. I don't imagine she'll be released any time soon."

"My God. That's awful."

"It is," Jenkins said. "But, unfortunately, it's not surprising. She has a history of mental illness. Has been heavily medicated for as long as I can remember. Have you met her?"

Ronnie knew he had to choose his words carefully. He didn't want to mention the stalking story for fear it would suggest a possible motive to the cop. A reason why he might want to terrorize her. "I just met her yesterday. Briefly."

"As I said, this is probably nothing, but I do have to follow it up. Esmerelda claims a chainsaw was terrorizing her all last night. Right below her bedroom window. Went on for some time, she claims. Two, three, four o'clock in the morning. We don't see any evidence of a chainsaw having been on her property, but who knows? Do you own a chainsaw?"

"Yeah."

"Were you using it last night?"

"I was clearing some dead trees in the forest. But that was in the afternoon. And we cut one standing-dead by the beach at about 8:30 last night, and then wrapped it up."

Jenkins scanned the property and pointed to Caleb's rented SUV. "You got some friends here."

"Yeah, still sleeping."

"It's not possible any of them had the chainsaw going late into the night?"

"No."

Jenkins paused briefly, scratched his forehead, and grinned. "Case closed. Just as I thought. Keep it between us, but what we have here is a clear-cut case of batshit-crazy. Unfortunately. Sorry to bother you."

"Not a problem," Ronnie said as the cop turned and headed toward his vehicle. The officer opened the car door, turned to Ronnie, and said. "One more thing."

Ronnie felt his face flush. "What's that?"

Jenkins smiled. "Welcome to the island."

As the cop drove away, Caleb opened the back porch screen door and scratched his head. His eyes were bloodshot, his brow furrowed. "What was that all about?"

As Caleb sat next to Ronnie on the porch, Ronnie relayed the story.

When he had finished, Caleb said, "Fuck, I slept through the siren and everything. Some soldier, eh?"

"You had a lot to drink."

"Tell me about it."

"Tell me something. Unless I'm mistaken, after you cut that standing-dead down, we cut it up and put Mister Stihl away. It wouldn't have been any later than nine. Am I right?"

"Yeah. I remember that much," Caleb said. "That was before I got pissed."

Ronnie sighed. He couldn't believe he'd been entertaining the possibility that Mister Stihl had acted alone. "And I put Mister Stihl in the pickup and put him in the barn last night after we got home. Right?"

Caleb sipped his coffee and furrowed his brow. "I remember you putting him in your truck. After that, I *assume* you drove him to the house and put him in the barn."

"I did. I know I did."

"Have you checked?"

"Not yet."

"Well, there's one way to find out."

Ronnie marched quickly over to the barn. As he entered, he spotted Mister Stihl and sighed deeply.

"He's here," he shouted to Caleb.

"Of course he is," Caleb said, reaching for the door. "I'm gonna start some breakfast. Fucking inbred lunatics around here. At least she's outta our hair."

Ronnie approached Mister Stihl and said soothingly, "Have you been a good boy?"

He touched the chain and winced, jerking his hand back swiftly.

Mister Stihl was hot to the touch.

Demon Rat

Cynthia Batista knew mentioning it would give everyone the impression she was crazy. Is that what she wanted them to think? Sitting in her living room gazing around at the guests enjoying after-dinner drinks, she wasn't sure. It was her dinner party, her quarterly shindig to be sure. Once every three months—on rare exceptions that rule for socialization would be broken—she would host a soirée. Return the favor, so to speak, for being invited to other get-togethers. She knew the protocol. If you wanted to see your friends in Charlottetown, Prince Edward Island (at least her friends), you had to give them at least a month's notice and plan a special dinner party. They'd arrive at five, stuff their faces, have a few and (only a few drinks), and be out the door by a respectable 7:30 pm. Two and a half hours of pure joy. Forget about spontaneity. Forget about really caring. Forget about deep feelings, deep connections. It all seemed so pretentious to her. So pretend. Maybe that's why she said it. Maybe she wanted to shock this group of garden-variety friends. Shock them out of their complacency and boring regimented lives.

Or maybe, now that she'd retired from her government job as a conservation officer and didn't have to answer to anybody, she just didn't care anymore. Life living up to other's expectations wasn't life at all.

Or maybe it was just the wine. After all, Cynthia was on her fifth glass and feeling a little tipsy.

Whatever the reason, she said it: "Hey, do you guys know I see cat ghosts all the time in my house?"

The mundane conversation became muted. The eyes of all five guests focused on Cynthia. There was Darin and Ruth Botacci, both Ontario transplants who'd sold their restaurant in favor of a more small-town and less stressful lifestyle. And Robert and Glenna Simonson, who'd up and quit their Alberta oilfield jobs in favor of a quaint little bed & breakfast. And finally, Ned Tesbitt, Cynthia's recently retired and recently acquired internet-dating-site boyfriend.

"Really?" Darin said.

Cynthia expected him to react first. He was a sarcastic bastard and often tried to goad people into saying stupid shit—only to center them out by laughing at them later. Of course, he played this game with the kindest of intentions—laughing *at* instead of laughing *with* his friends.

"Yeah," Cynthia said. "They were here when I moved in. Sometimes I see them at night. They scare the hell out of my real cats at times. Other times, they play nice together."

"Do you talk to them?" Darin said. "Do they talk to you?"

A short and barely audible giggle or two. Then silence.

"Cats don't talk, silly," Cynthia said. "At least not with human voices. Although my real cats, Lucy and Brandy, certainly know how to communicate with me in cat-speak. No, I just see the ghosts sometimes at night. Maybe sitting on the couch. Sometimes on my bed. Sometimes roaming around. You guys probably don't believe me, and that's fine. I guess it comes down to whether you believe in ghosts or not. I know I do."

Darin scratched his thick grey beard and crossed his legs, striking a psychiatrist pose. "And how long has this been going on, exactly? This seeing-ghost-cats behavior."

Laughter.

Cynthia waited for it to die down. "You don't have to believe me. If you don't believe in ghosts, you definitely won't believe in ghost cats."

"I believe in ghosts," Ned, a retired architect, said.

"That's one," Cynthia said, gulping a mouthful of red wine. "How many others?"

Brandy, Cynthia's black cat, stealthily moved down the stairs and into the living room. She eyeballed the guests, meowed, spun around, and darted up the stairs.

"Look," Ruth said, squeezing Darin's leg. "I think Brandy just saw a ghost."

Uproarious laughter.

Ruth certainly knew how to pick up a bouncing ball and roll with it, taking over where her husband Darin had left off.

"Seriously," Cynthia said. "How many of you guys believe in ghosts? Let's have a show of hands."

Ned's hand was the first to go up, but Cynthia already knew he was on board, if for no other reason than to come to her defense as her partner.

Glenna wiped away a wispy grey hair and raised her hand. "I believe in ghosts. I know Robert is on the fence about it, but I do."

"I'm neutral," Robert said, scratching a thick red mustache. "I don't believe. I don't disbelieve."

Turning to Darin and Ruth, Cynthia said, "What about you guys?"

"All seriousness aside," Ruth said, scratching her sunken cheek. "Sorry, I meant all joking aside, I do believe in ghosts.

I've never seen a cat ghost, but I have seen apparitions of people." She slowly raised her hand.

Gazing around at the group, Darin's brow wrinkled, as if everyone was waiting for him to weigh in. Maybe it was time to kiss his wife's ass. "Honestly..."

"What does that mean?" Cynthia blurted. "That everything you've told us so far is bullshit?"

Ned brought his hand to his mouth, but not before a small laugh escaped. His beady eyes scanned the group as he scratched his thinning grey hair.

After a momentary and awkward silence, Darin said, "It's just an expression. Maybe not a very good one. What I was trying to say before I was interrupted is I'm with Rob. I'm neutral." He thrust his hand in the air. "No. I've changed my mind. Your cat ghost story convinced me. Now I'm all in. I believe in ghosts. It's an epiphany."

Everyone laughed. Well, almost everyone. Ned and Cynthia didn't. Ned even moved a little closer to Cynthia and put a comforting hand on her shoulder. She smiled a little and placed her hand on his knee.

"I'm just kidding," Darin said. "Actually, I *am* neutral."

Grabbing her husband's hand, Glenna stood, pulling him up. Then, after a long, mouth-covering yawn, she said, "I guess the spooky talk will have to wait. We're old and boring and have to leave now. Thanks so much for the lovely dinner and lovely company."

It was like a dog whistle. In seconds, the two couples were at the door donning their jackets, offering perfunctory thanks, mechanical handshakes, and obligatory hugs. Then they were gone, and a few minutes later, Ned and Cynthia, illuminated by a coffee-table candle, sat holding hands on a comfy loveseat. Cynthia sipped wine. Ned sipped water.

Since they'd begun dating two months ago, he had spent the odd night at her Charlottetown house. But today was Sunday and he'd told her earlier he could make her dinner shindig—marking the first time he'd met her friends—but had things to do Monday so would not be spending the night.

"What do you think of them?" Cynthia asked, squeezing his hand tighter.

"They seem nice."

***

After Ned had left, Cynthia put a few dishes in the dishwasher, put some leftovers in the fridge, and turned in for the night. She wasn't a big drinker and the wine had made her tired and dozy. After a brief analysis of the ghost cat story and how poorly it had been received, she found sleep tugging at her heavy eyelids. Eventually, she drifted off into a deep sleep.

A few hours later, she was startled awake by a loud *thunk*.

She bolted upright in bed and glanced around the bedroom. In the suffused blue nightlight plugged into an outlet beside her dresser, she could see enough to realize her cats hadn't joined her in bed as they usually did. That was odd. Her eyes moved around the room and then stopped at an object at the foot of her bed.

It was a giant rat. Flat on its back. Extremities outstretched. Appearing quite dead.

She stifled a scream and flew out of bed as a shot of adrenaline shattered the residual cobwebs of sleep. In spite of her rising fear, she moved closer to the rat. As she approached, it flipped over on all fours, spread its legs, and floated above the bed. As it rose, it grew. By the time it reached the ceiling, it covered the entire ceiling.

Its huge red eyes studied her. It grinned. A large drop of saliva dropped from its open mouth, splashing onto the floor like a bucket of ice-cold water.

"Aaaaaaaaaaaaaahhhhh!" she screamed, dashing for the door. But as she reached it, she stopped, glanced up, and saw the massive rat vanish through the ceiling.

Five minutes later, calm enough to sip herbal tea but not calm enough to re-enter her bedroom, she sat cuddled up on the living room sofa with her cats, Brandy and Lucy. She had a flashlight in her hand and occasionally she would illuminate a dark corner of her house, fearing the rat had returned. But each time she shone the light, she saw nothing out of the ordinary.

A dark shadow resembling a cat crossed the living room floor. Lucy and Brandy did not stir from their attention-seeking poses.

Cynthia smiled. Last night, she hadn't had time to tell her guests that her favorite ghost cat was Shadow, the friendly one, yet perhaps paradoxically, also the warrior.

Without hesitation, she said, "Shadow, go upstairs and make sure that fucking demon rat is gone. Send it where you want, but get it the hell out of my house."

***

"Ghost cats," Darin said, staring at the glowing full moon from his bedroom window. "I've never heard of anything so stupid in my entire life."

"Tell me about it, honey," Ruth said from her prostrate position in bed. "I was just humoring her and you took me seriously."

"Well, I thought you were, but I wanted to go neutral anyway. She cooked a nice dinner for us. Didn't want to piss her off."

"Are you kidding?" Ruth said. "Did you see the look on her face when you struck that psychiatrist pose? I'd call that daggers of contempt."

"Really? I didn't think I upset her that much."

"She's pretty serious about the supernatural. And highly superstitious."

"Well, I think it's a bunch of bullshit for weak-minded and gullible people."

"So do I, sweetie. Now come to bed."

As Darin began to close the cloth curtains, something caught his eye. A black spot on the moon. Or was it in front of the moon? He stopped, parted the blinds, and watched it, suddenly scared. The black shadow grew legs, a head, eyes, ears, and a fang-filled mouth.

Backing away from the window, Darin wiped his eyes. *No, it can't be.*

But it was. Instantly the rat ballooned in size and propelled itself like a nuclear-powered rocket straight toward the window.

"Oh my fucking God," Darin said, scrambling underneath the bed quickly and covering his eyes.

Ruth climbed out of bed, knelt down, and peered underneath it. "What the hell is wrong with you?"

"Run... baby... run. It's coming!"

Ruth spun around and looked at the window. "What's comi... "

The window shattered. Shards of glass flew everywhere.

Ruth instinctively bent down, shielding her face from the propellants. "Yaaaaaaaeeeeeeeeeeeeee!!!"

Thunk!

Petrified with terror, Darin managed to crawl out from underneath the bed, take his wife by the hand, and tug her toward the door. "We gotta get out of here."

He opened the door quickly, spun around, and looked back.

An oversized rat was crouched on the floor, red laser-beam eyes drilling into him. Its mouth opened, exposing large fangs. It grinned and attacked.

Darin pushed his wife through the door. "Come on, honey. Hurry, it's after us."

Halfway down the stairs, Ruth, her voice edged with panic, said, "What? What's after us?"

"It's a demon rat... A FUCKING DEMON RAT!!"

***

Six days later, out of the blue, Cynthia decided to call Glenna. She craved more spontaneity in her life and was growing tired of living a prescribed existence. Besides, she knew Glenna believed in ghosts—at least she'd said as much—and she wanted to get something off her chest. At 7:36 pm that evening—exactly the same time four of her guests had departed her dinner party almost a week ago—she dialed Glenna's number.

Glenna picked up on the first ring.

Cynthia dispensed with the social niceties in short order and paused, waiting to see if Glenna would take the bait.

She did. "You see any ghost cats lately?"

"Yeah," Cynthia said. "I saw Shadow not long ago. The same night you guys were over for dinner. I didn't get a chance to tell you the last time, but Shadow is the friendly one. He's also a warrior."

An uncomfortable silence.

"Oh, really?" Glenna said.

"Yeah, and something else."

"What's that?

"A demon rat came into my bedroom and Shadow chased him away. And I had a terrible nightmare last night that Shadow sent the demon rat to terrorize Darin and Ruth. You heard from them lately?"

"No, but I'm sure they're fine."

"I hope so. In my dream, the demon rat smashed through their bedroom window."

Another uncomfortable silence.

"Listen," Glenna said. "I'd really love to hear this story, but I'm right in the middle of something right now. Can we talk tomorrow?"

***

Two hours later, Glenna went into her bedroom, slipped into her nightgown, and turned to her husband Robert, who was reading a novel. "You wouldn't believe who called me earlier? And you wouldn't believe what she said?"

She relayed the phone conversation to Robert.

After she'd finished, he closed his book. "I'm sure Darin and Ruth are just fine. You shouldn't have told her you believe in ghosts, dear. Now she thinks she's got a sympathetic ear."

Glenna scratched her cheek and approached the window. "Well, I think it's a bunch of bullshit for weak-minded and gullible people."

"So do I, sweetie. Now come to bed."

Repression

Sebastian Greenwood hated the C word. Commitment. Wearing your heart on your sleeve, relinquishing your freedom to cow-tow to someone else's whims and desires. Wasn't that the reason for the seven-year itch? The high divorce rate? People weren't designed to mate for life. Inevitably, as everyone knows, familiarity breeds contempt.

At least that was what he was thinking about as he weaved his way through early evening traffic in Calgary, enroute to Dolly Peterson's home for dinner and maybe a glass or two of wine. They'd been seeing each other for almost two years now and Sebastian, a young 55, at least in his own mind, had managed to masterfully avoid that dreaded C word. Sure, there had been a few close calls but he'd always succeeded at steering the conversation carefully away from the landmines and well into demilitarized zones. Friendly zones, friendly fire.

"I don't know what this is?" Dolly had asked one day, brushing back a lock of blonde hair and arching an eyebrow at him. "What is this? What are we?"

"We're really close," Sebastian had said. "Really, really close."

"What, you mean close as in good friends? You mean close as in good friends with benefits? You mean close as in boyfriend and girlfriend? What do you mean?"

"I used to think I wasn't relationship material, but with you, babe, it could be different."

After a long and contemplative pause, Dolly had decided against poking the bear. She'd decided to give him the benefit of the doubt and allow him more time to work through his feelings. Hoping, perhaps, that his feelings for her would catch up to where her feelings were for him.

There were a few other examples of Dolly wanting to know, asking precisely where he stood on "us."

But Sebastian didn't have time to mull them over right now. He'd arrived at Dolly's suburban home in Evergreen, a new and popular Calgary residential subdivision where every cookie-cutter home looked almost exactly like the one beside it—or the one at the end of the block for that matter.

He quickly checked his reflection in the rear-view mirror. He liked what he saw. Very few wrinkles. A good set of teeth. A full head of mid-length slicked-back black hair. Emerald-green eyes that some people said were his best and most captivating feature. He ran a hand through his jell-coated head and flattened down what was already like spaghetti stuck to a wall. He smiled and exited his Audi Quattro, a company car and one of the perks of being a highly paid pharmaceutical sales rep.

***

Dinner, beef lasagna and Caesar salad, was simple yet delicious. The ice-cold Chilean white wine, slightly fruity, slightly sweet, was going down like Kool-Aid on a hot summer day. Even though it was the beginning of fall. The conversation, extra special. Not too serious, not too silly. Just the right superficial mix for Sebastian's particular palate.

"Would you like dessert?" Dolly asked, scooping up two dinner plates and cutlery.

"No, thanks. I'm sweet enough."

She left the dining room and went into the kitchen, clanged the dishes into the dishwasher, and spun around. "Are you?"

Oh, oh. The landmine. I stepped on it. Gonna blow my foot off. "Sweet enough for you I hope."

Dolly returned and swept the salad bowls and some cutlery from the table. She bent down as if to blow out a candle, then changed her mind and returned to the kitchen. "Are you?"

"Am I what?"

"Don't play dumb, Sebastian."

Change the subject. "That dinner was delicious."

"Don't change the subject. Do you think you're sweet enough for me?"

"I thought so, otherwise I wouldn't be with you."

Her blue eyes had turned into razor-sharp daggers. She stomped out of the kitchen and sat down next to him. "You're not with me. You never were. You've never given me any kind of commitment. You're afraid of commitment. You're in this halfway and just when it suits you. Just when you want to get laid or want some company."

"Come on, baby. I'm fond of you. You know that."

Her eyes flashed. Her cheeks flushed. A vein in her neck popped and pulsated. "People are fond of goldfish. You can't say you love me. I'll give you a hint, Sebastian, for future reference, if some significant other tells you they love you don't say likewise. It's the most infuriating thing in the world for a woman to hear."

"I'm sorry," he said. "Nothing else came to mind." Gone was his quick wit and charm. Or was it manipulation? Perhaps gaslighting?

"Don't apologize. Why should you apologize for feelings you don't have. When I go into a relationship, I'm all in. We've been together long enough. I've given you plenty of rope, plenty of time to see if you could ever develop feelings for me. You haven't. Maybe you're incapable of such emotions. Maybe you don't want them in your life. Maybe I'm not your type. Whatever it is, I'm tired of your bullshit. Tired of you. Why do you even keep me around, Sebastian? You're a good-looking, successful guy. You could find someone. Find someone that you can connect with. Or, maybe you can't because you're too afraid of intimacy. Too afraid of commitment. I'll bet you hate the fucking C word."

"Come on, honey. You know I love you."

Dolly's eyes narrowed and her lips tightened. "Don't say that word unless you mean it!"

Sebastian stood. "I think it's time for me to go."

"Maybe there is something you *are* good at," Dolly said. "Reading my fucking mind. Now get out!"

***

An hour later, Sebastian stood on the balcony of his fifth floor, inner-city condo gazing at the glittering city lights. Some of the sadness, some of the disappointment, and some of the depression had passed. Reason began to prevail.

She's right. For the last two years, she's had expectations that one day I would return to her the love she's shown for me. She's had hope. She's had dreams. She's loved me to the core, accepted my faults, supported me in every way, and what have I given back? A little support, a lot of good fucks, and a lot of bullshit or just downright clever manipulation and evasiveness.

It started to dawn on Sebastian that he'd been dating a ticking time bomb. One that he'd manufactured, even setting the timer to the precise second of detonation. And detonate it had. It was simple really. She doesn't get what she wants. Instead of confronting it, she represses it. Then when her love is not reciprocated she gets resentful. Then she gets angry. Then she gets sad. Then she gets critical. Then she gets insulting. Then she gets contemptuous. Then she gets malicious. A string of small explosions leading up to one massive explosion. *But, wait a minute. The contempt and maliciousness haven't arrived yet. They're there, alright, bubbling beneath the surface. Maybe they'll explode next time, if they'll ever be a next time.*

He sighed and washed it down with a gulp of beer. "What a fuck-up I am."

And he *was*. He'd led her on. He'd played with her emotions. He'd used her. He knew now as he knew then; she wasn't the one for him. Yes, he did love her. Loved her as a friend. But she loved him as a boyfriend. And if he was a real man, he would've told her that a long time ago, spared her the heartache, spared her the grief, before, not after, she'd fallen in love with him.

He stopped grinding his teeth. "What a fucking shit I really am."

He climbed onto his balcony railing. Stood on the edge, a beer in one hand, the other hand clinging to the corner of the concrete high-rise. It had begun to drizzle.

He looked down below. *A long way down. No surviving that.* He started stepping away from the comforting concrete and slipped on the wet railing. He teetered, stepped sideways, and grabbed the wall for support. His heart raced. His throat went dry. He began sweating.

He watched a man wearing a long black trench coat stagger down the street. The man stopped and looked up. "Jump." The man continued on down the street.

Fucking insensitive asshole. Just like me. Maybe he's right. "Fuck you!"

The man stopped. "Jump, you fucking pussy. You that much of a loser that you can't get your own death right. Fuck you and the shit you rode in on."

Sebastian climbed down from the balcony and tossed his half-full beer can over the edge. It landed with a splat directly in front of the man, who only stood and glared at Sebastian with large eyes that seemed to flash blood-red for just an instant.

"It's 'ship' you rode in on, dummy," Sebastian said.

"Come down here and mouth off to me, you fucking pussy," the man said.

Sebastian stepped into his condo quickly and closed the sliding-glass door. He went into the chrome kitchen, grabbed another beer from the fridge, went into his office, and sat down at his computer. He drank half the beer in three gulps, formulated his thoughts, and then began writing an email.

Dear Dolly,

I'm sorry for the way I've treated you over the last two years. You were right to explode on me tonight. I deserved it. You've been repressing your emotions for all this time and they had to explode some time because I wasn't reciprocating your love for me. I thought when I first met you that we had the right chemistry in all the ways necessary to forge a strong, intimate, loving, and trusting relationship. I realized after only a few months that it wasn't there for me and I should've told you then to spare you all the heartache and grief.

Maybe it wasn't there because I just didn't see the chemistry. Maybe it wasn't there simply because of me. You were also right when you said I'm afraid of commitment. Maybe that's been the problem all along and it has nothing to do with you. When I think about it, I've blown up all of my past relationships ultimately because of my fear of commitment.

Where did it come from? Not from my mother. Not from my father. They did everything right. I guess I've managed to shut it up and repress it for all these years, but when I really think about it now, it dates back to a childhood sweetheart I had. Puppy love, teenage love, high school sweetheart, all that stuff. I had a girlfriend called Graciella. Long story short, she dumped me for the class president and during all of my high school years paraded him around in front of me like a trophy. I almost dropped out of high school because of it. After I graduated from high school, I became sad and depressed and eventually bitter about relationships. I became afraid to put my heart on my sleeve only to have the sleeve torn into pathetic little pieces by a woman. I took out my anger toward Graciella on the whole female species. It's my fuck-up. I own it.

I need help.

I hope at some point you can find it in your heart to forgive me for all the suffering I've caused you. I don't think that's what I intended. But, if I have to be completely honest with myself, maybe on some level, I did intend it. Maybe I intended to punish you for what Graciella did to me. I know, right? Pretty fucked up.

After all these years of living with and repressing my shit, I think I've finally figured out a way to fix it. I hope I meet you in the afterlife, Dolly. I hope you forgive me in the afterlife. I hope we can be friends in the afterlife.

Wishing you all the best that life has to offer. I hope you find a man who appreciates you for who you are and reciprocates your love for him. You deserve it. You're an amazing and very caring person.

Lots of love, Sebastian.

Sebastian pressed SEND and calmly closed his laptop. It felt good to finally get his own shit off his chest and own it. It was liberating.

He walked casually to his balcony door and swung it open. He then took ten steps back, stopped, and charged the balcony with all the speed he could muster. He hit the railing with both hands and vaulted over it and into the air. As he plunged swiftly down to the sidewalk below, what went through his mind was nothing resembling the stories he'd heard about near-death experiences. No white light. His whole life wasn't flashing before his eyes. There was just a single thought replaying in his mind over and over again like a broken record.

I'm a fuck-up and then I die.

I'm a fuck-up and then I die...

***

Relaxing on a plush leather couch and reading a self-help book in a downtown coffee shop almost a year later, Sebastian no longer took anything for granted. He knew it was a miracle that he'd survived his suicide attempt. He'd landed on a small vinyl awning above the condo entrance. Although he'd crashed through it, broken both legs and one arm, the awning had broken his fall and saved his life. Strange thing was, the awning was nowhere near his fall trajectory. Somehow he'd managed to drift left in mid-flight and strike the awning. But Sebastian knew it had nothing to do with "somehow."

God had intervened, saved his life, and given him a second chance.

He was now a born-again Christian.

He saw a shrink regularly.

He didn't drink.

He attended group therapy.

He volunteered at the local food bank.

And, just last month, he'd gotten off his anti-depression medication.

Although still single, he now had hope. One by one he was confronting his inner demons and releasing them into the atmosphere.

Even his boss at the pharmaceutical company had been understanding, granting him a one-year leave of absence to "get your shit together." He would be returning to his job next week, the one-year anniversary of his suicide attempt.

"Do you think that'll work for the likes of you?"

The voice startled him. He looked up and saw she was eyeing the book he was reading: *How to Have a Successful Relationship,* by Jason Legend.

Maybe it was the residual and deleterious withdrawal effects of quitting the anti-depressants, but he didn't recognize her right away. "I hope so. I just started it, but I hear it's a good book."

"It *is*, actually," the blonde woman said. "I've read it."

Suddenly, he did recognize her. "Dolly?"

"Do you mind?" she asked, pointing to an armchair across from him.

"Please do," he said. "How are you?"

She sat down. "I'm not gonna mince words. I got your email. Thanks for admitting the error of your ways. I appreciate that. I learned that you had survived your suicide attempt. Read about it in the paper. I'm sorry, I couldn't bring myself to contact you or visit you in the hospital."

"Hey, no apologies necessary. I understand. I'm the one who should be apologizing."

"You already have. And I accept it."

"Thanks. I'm really sorry."

"Don't," she said, her eyes moistening. "It wasn't all your fault. I saw the signs early on and I should've acted on them. Should've dumped you long before everything festered like it did. Love is blind. And stupid at times."

"Are you okay, now?"

"I don't know. I kind of hate men right now, but at least I'm working on getting over it." She pointed to the book. "Like you."

Sebastian frowned, realizing for the first time the extent of the damage he'd done. He'd not only managed to manufacture a time bomb, but he'd managed to transfer his hatred of women to Dolly, who now hated men. He'd created a monster. *But, wait.* She was working on it. Like he was. There was hope.

"I hope you find it in your heart to forgive me for my part in... your dislike of men."

"As I said, I'm working on it. And, don't give yourself so much credit. It wasn't only you. It was other exes, some before you, some after you."

"Can you forgive me?"

A single tear sprouted on her left eye and she quickly dabbed it away with her shirtsleeve. "Yes, I forgive you. I know it's unhealthy to harbor hate. At least that's what my shrink says. At least that's what I've read."

"You're not in a relationship now?"

"No, not for the last six months. How about you?"

"No. I'm still working on my own shit." Sebastian listed all the changes he'd made since the attempted suicide.

Dolly finally smiled. "Wow. That *is* impressive. I'm happy for you." She stood. "Sorry. I really should be going."

"It's been great seeing you," Sebastian said. "And I wish you the best."

She turned to leave. "Likewise."

"Dolly?"

She stopped and spun around. "Yeah?"

"Do you think there's a chance that one day we might be friends?"

"I don't know. You have my number. It's still the same. Give me a few more months of recovery and then maybe give me a call. We'll see what happens."

***

The over-riding emotion that Sebastian felt as he entered his condo was hope. Dolly had accepted his apology. Even though, whether intentionally or not, she'd replied with the same word he'd used so often in the past when she used to tell him she loved him. 'Likewise,' albeit in a slightly different context. He'd wished her the best and she'd responded with 'likewise.' Was it true? Did the scars from the wounds he'd inflicted run that deep? Would they ever heal? *Yes, they will. Mine did. Mine are. There's hope. She'll get better and I hope we can be friends again.*

He sat down on his couch and ruminated about his relationship with Dolly. After surviving the fall, he couldn't bring himself to contact her. Hadn't felt he deserved her friendship, never mind forgiveness. The guilt had been overwhelming. Now, at least everything was out in the open. She'd accepted his apology. She'd forgiven him. With a little more time and space, perhaps a friendship could flourish again.

He went down the list of all the positive changes he'd made in his life over the last year. He truly was on a path toward redemption.

A little later, feeling all warm and fuzzy and happy, he decided a small celebration was in order. He went to his fridge, opened it, and looked inside. A one-year-old lone Budweiser can stared back at him.

How long is the shelf life for beer? He was about to find out. He reached inside, grabbed it, and cracked it open, forgetting all about the expiry date, even though he believed there was one. He wasn't worried about falling off the wagon. He hadn't touched a drink in almost a year because his psychiatrist had warned him that the anti-depressants didn't mix well with alcohol. Even in his heyday, he only drank on weekends; and then usually no more than two or three drinks. Booze was the least of his problems. And he wasn't on the medication anymore. *So who cares?*

Reclining on his balcony, he took the first sip. *Not bad. Cheers to me. Cheers to Dolly. Please God, grant her the peace, happiness, and fulfillment in life that she so richly deserves. Please God, forgive me for my part in her unhappiness, suffering, and issues. Thank you, my Lord and Savior, for answering my prayers. Amen.*

A light drizzle began.

Sebastian watched the dimly lit street below. A man dressed in a black trench coat walked purposefully down the street, stopped below his apartment, and said: "Remember me, you fucking pussy? Just like I thought. Such a loser you couldn't even manage to get your own death right."

Cold tentacles of fear gripped the nape of Sebastian's neck, plunging down into his heart like a frozen dagger.

From inside of his trench coat, the man produced an assault rifle and aimed it at Sebastian.

A red laser beam danced across Sebastian's forehead. "No!"

The man fired.

Kaplow!

Halls of Madness

"Yes, I'm gonna get you."

"No, you're not."

"Yes, I'm gonna get you."

"You can't get me. You're dead."

"Oh, but I'm not. I'm back. I live anywhere. I live everywhere."

"You're dead. Go away."

"I won't go away until you succumb to your fate."

"It's not real. You're not real."

"Oh, but you know I am."

Reality, reality, snap back into reality. Zachariah Middlecoff opened his eyes and realized for the first time that morning that he wasn't in his private room. No. He was sitting on the floor leaning against the wall of the fluorescently lit white hallway. He'd lost a gap of time. How much time? He scanned the hall, half-expecting Zimeon, the black-suited monster, to burst through one of the many doors at any second and drag him deep down into the black abyss where Zimeon resided.

But, he didn't see Zimeon. He sighed, choking back the lump of fear that was rising up his throat.

He saw a thin, middle-aged woman with long, straggly grey hair standing and facing the wall. Talking to it. Was she talking to Zimeon? "I won't let you out. No. I won't let you out. You don't play nice. Why don't you play nice?"

She banged her head against the wall repeatedly until blood started spraying everywhere.

Pushing against the wall with his legs and back, Zach got to his feet. *Get to your room. Now.* He snaked past her quickly as two orderlies rushed past him with a stretcher, grabbed the woman, and began strapping her into it.

She offered little protest: "He doesn't play nice. I don't want to play with him."

"You're hurting yourself, Agnes," one orderly said. "Don't hurt yourself."

They whisked her off in the opposite direction and Zach carried on. He passed two doors and stopped at door number three. Actually, number 23. *Is this my room? What number is my room?*

The door was slightly ajar. Zach pushed it open and looked inside.

An old man wearing a white hospital gown greeted him with a wide grin. "This isn't your room. It's my room."

"Where's my room?"

The man flung open his hospital gown, exposing his nakedness. "How the hell should I know? Get out of here. Leave me alone."

For a second, Zach thought he saw Zimeon's black suit underneath the white gown. The monster's black suit. He blinked repeatedly and backed up. No. It was only the man's shriveled penis.

"Piss on you," the man said, grabbing his penis, approaching Zach, and spraying a stream of urine at him.

Zach slammed the door and continued down the hall. Three doors down, he saw an elderly man sitting at a table by himself. On the table was a chess board full of chess pieces. An empty chair sat across from the man.

"Checkmate," the man declared as Zach passed, slamming a king down so hard the board shook and pieces rolled and rattled to the floor. "Now look what you've gone and done. You're a sore loser, you know that? Can't you play nice? Can't you be a good sport?"

Zach shuffled along, kicking a few chess pieces toward the man. *Where the hell is my room? Better find it before Zimeon finds me.* He arrived at a T in the maze of hallways and stopped, scratching his stringy grey hair, and looking furtively left, then right, left, then right.

Which way? He was about to go left but then chose right. *Must be that way.* He walked about thirty feet, stopped, and squinted. He saw a tiny black ball far away, perhaps thirty rooms or more. Maybe a full city block. It began hurling toward him like a Category 5 hurricane.

"Yes, I'm gonna get you."

"No, you're not."

"Yes, I'm gonna get you."

"You can't get me. You're dead."

"Oh, but I'm not. I'm back. I live anywhere. I live everywhere."

"You're dead. Go away."

But Zimeon wasn't going away. He was out for blood. Zach looked around frantically for a weapon, any weapon. Nothing. *But wait, a door. A closet door.* He reefed on it. It creaked but didn't budge. Panic rattled his nerves. A ball of fear shot up his throat, acidic fowl-tasting bile. Suddenly fueled by an adrenaline surge of superhuman strength, he tugged hard on the door and it snapped open, shattering the wooden door hinges, wood chips flying everywhere. He pulled it open, grabbing the first thing his hand felt—a mop.

He tucked it behind his back and leaned against the door.

Twenty feet in front of him, the black hurricane stopped. It spun around ferociously for a few seconds, hurling debris everywhere.

Zach shielded his face with his arm. "No, no, no. Please, no. Go away. You're dead."

The sound and the fury precipitously stopped.

Zach slid his arm partially away from his face and snuck a look, deathly afraid and yet knowing what he would see.

Black suit, black shirt, black tie, black shoes. And the ugliest looking black head he'd ever laid eyes on. Full of matted fur. Blood-red, devilish eyes. And that shit-eating, horse-toothed grin.

Zimeon said, "You're a long way from home, Zach. You lost? You need to come with me."

Zach reacted quickly, gripping the mop tightly in both hands and smashing Zimeon in the side of the head so hard the mop handle snapped in two. But it had the desired outcome. The beast staggered back, slamming his head on a doorframe, wobbling, and then withering down the wall.

Zach seized the opportunity, flipping the broken handle in the air and catching it with the splintered and broken, razor-sharp business end pointing out. An improvised spear. He knelt down in front of the monster, gripped the mop handle tightly in both hands, and raised it high in the air.

Beep... beep... beep... beeeeeeeeeeeeeeeeeeeeeeeep... beep... beep!

The sound of the alarm startled him and he froze as panic seized up his extremities. Four orderlies, men in white, raced down the hall toward him. He looked down at his foe.

The black suit transformed into a white lab coat with a breast pocket full of pens. The vicious head morphed into the small head and chiseled facial features of a man with a disheveled black comb-over, twisted black-framed glasses, and blood gushing from the side of his head.

He read the silver-colored name tag pinned to the man's chest: *Doctor Milo Stanford, Chief Psychiatrist.*

He dropped the mop handle, sprang to his feet, spun around, and bolted down the hall. *No, no, no, what the fuck did I do? Not the padded room. Not the straitjacket. Not the ankle and wrist bracelets. Not solitary. Not the hole. Not the black abyss. I can't take it anymore. It'll drive me crazy. What the fuck did I do?*

***

One month later.

Sheldon McConnell thought the halls looked inordinately sterile for a sportswear manufacturer. White walls. Ceiling-mounted fluorescent lights every eight feet. Drab grey floors. He'd just gotten off the elevator, arriving at the sixth floor where owner and CEO Deloris Jacoby kept an office from which she presided over her Vancouver-based, medium-sized clothing company, Jacoby Style & Sportswear.

"Never mind," he muttered, hearing a slight echo as he headed to the end of the hall. "Just get the damn job."

"Damn job... damn job," the halls said.

A door opened to his right and a young man with a mop of long brown hair stepped out, his arms full of hangers, the hangers full of articles of clothing. The man eyed him up and down. "Did you say something?"

"No," Sheldon lied. He was applying for a job as a sportswear salesman and the last thing he wanted before he even got in the door to the interview was for Jacoby employees to think he was crazy.

The man gave him a puzzled look, turned, and shuffled down the hall.

Sheldon reached the end of the hall, was about to knock, and then noticed the sign: *The office of Jacoby Style & Sportswear CEO Deloris Jacoby. Please come in.*

He opened the door and stepped inside and was greeted by a young and attractive brunette secretary, conservatively dressed in a black knee-length skirt, white blouse, and black blazer. Her black-framed glasses accentuated the efficient-and-sexy secretary stereotype.

"You must be Sheldon," she said, rising from her desk and thrusting out her hand with a bright smile. "I'm Bonnie Tiller. You can call me Tilly."

Sheldon shook the offered hand. Soft. Smooth. Warm. *Wow. Nickname basis already and I haven't even gotten the job.* "Nice to meet you."

"The pleasure is all mine." She gestured to a closed door behind her desk. "Go right in. Mrs. Jacoby is expecting you. Good luck."

Shelden entered and closed the door behind him. He saw a desk near a wall of windows, affording a nice view of the downtown cityscape. Two chairs were in front of the desk. A living room of sorts was set up to the left; a couch, coffee table, and two armchairs. Beside it, racks of clothing and clothed mannequins.

The woman, her black-grey hair tied neatly back in a bun, sat flipping through pages of a document, her eyes glued to it. Without looking up, she said. "Take a seat, please. I'll be right with you."

Sheldon sat. "Thanks."

He watched her as she read, trying not to stare. She looked to be in her fifties, but had aged well. Dainty and thin features. Small crow's feet around her eyes, but otherwise soft, smooth, supple topographies. She too wore a black blazer and a bright red blouse. Sheldon couldn't be sure, but he thought he'd noticed black pants in contrast to Tilly's stylish skirt.

After an uncomfortable silence, at least for Sheldon, she raised her Emerald-green eyes from the pages and extended her left, wedding-ring-appointed, hand. "Nice to meet you."

Sheldon took it and shook it. Firm grip. Slightly clammy. "Good to meet you."

She pushed the thick manuscript aside, opened a drawer of her desk, and pulled out two stapled eggshell-colored pages. Sheldon's resume. She scanned both pages quickly, set it down on the desk, and bored straight into Sheldon's eyes without blinking. Alright, Sheldon. Do you mind if I call you that?"

"No."

Then she asked the one question Sheldon hoped she wouldn't: "I see you've had a fair amount of sales experience, but how do you explain that one-year gap in your job history?"

Sheldon shifted in his seat. He felt a bead of perspiration drop from his armpit and trickle down his side. *How do you explain the halls and walls of misery, sadness, and depression that close in on you after you learn your mother and father, brother and sister, burned to death in a freak house fire? How do you explain the loneliness and despair that cuts you off from the outside world and transforms you into a feeble and introverted shell of the man you once were? How do you explain telling your old unsympathetic boss at the used car lot to 'Go fuck yourself?'*

"You tell the truth, that's how."

"My... my family died in a house fire caused by faulty electrical wiring. I had to take some time off to recover." *That's it, keep it short and simple, stupid.*

"I'm sorry to hear that," Delores said in a conciliatory tone. "Do you think you've recovered enough to work for us?"

Sheldon nodded. "Thank you. I think so."

Her eyes returned to the resume. "As I said, I see some good sales history here." Her index finger stopped near the bottom of the second page. "But what's this? You worked as a hospital porter? Transferring patients to the morgue?"

"That was part of the job," Sheldon said. "Among other duties, as I've outlined there. I paid my way through university with that job."

Her eyes met his full on. "You mean you didn't take out a student loan to fund your education?"

"No."

"You worked full-time and attended university full-time?"

"Yes, Mrs. Jacoby."

She smiled and scratched her nose. "Hmm. That *is* impressive. Most students are in massive debt nowadays by the time they finish university."

"I don't carry any debt."

"Good to hear. How old did you say you were?"

He hadn't, but he didn't bother correcting her. "Thirty-three."

"Any significant other in your life?"

Maybe a little personal. Yeah, right, after what you just told her. "No, ma'am."

After a momentary silence, in which she seemed to be studying him for some sign of a crack in the mold, she opened her desk drawer and filed the resume away. "Let me tell you a little bit about the company and what I expect of you."

Sheldon folded his hands together, leaned forward, and crossed his legs. "Okay."

"I prefer people who can think outside of the box," she said. "I demand honesty, integrity, and loyalty. But if you think I'm wrong about something, don't be afraid to tell me. Two heads are typically better than one."

Sheldon nodded, a satisfied smile beginning to form.

As she told the story of how she'd brought Jacoby from a fledgling operation in the basement suite of a house to a successful thirty-five employee sportswear design and manufacturing company that now owned the impressive building from which it operated, Sheldon only half-listened. He couldn't help the feeling of elation creeping over him. He was sure she was gonna hire him.

"But I can't take full responsibility for Jacoby's meteoric rise to the top," she said. "I have a team of loyal employees around me, some who've been rewarded with shares in the company, very lucrative profit-sharing structures. One of the reasons most companies fail is they don't reward their talent properly. The talent subsequently feels underappreciated and begins to look for greener pastures. I've only had five employees leave in five years. Two were for personal reasons and the other three, well, let's just say that maybe they got a little too greedy."

She paused and Sheldon felt as if he needed to say something. "That *is* impressive."

She grinned. "I like to think so. Now, let's get to the point, shall we? What qualities do you think you could bring to our team to elevate our success even further?"

Sheldon had anticipated the question and had rehearsed it several times. It flowed from his lips like water off a duck's back: "I'm hard-working, loyal, honest, smart, and creative."

He thought of throwing in "team player" as icing on the cake but ultimately overturned the idea, believing it would come off as corny. And besides, he preferred his independence and was a much better self-starter than team player. No point in bullshitting at this point in the game. Honesty had gotten him this far.

"You're beginning to sound like the right person for the job," Delores said. "But there's one more thing I need to ask you?"

Sheldon felt a lump in his throat. The nape of his neck suddenly felt cold. "Go ahead, ma'am."

"You wouldn't be replacing anybody. We've just been growing so fast that we need more sales people. One of the big contracts we just landed is with The Institute. Do you know of it?"

Sheldon had lived in Vancouver long enough to know The Institute. At one time, it was a short-term psychiatric care hospital where most patients would get treated and released. That had been about ten years ago. Since then it had been remodeled and renamed and most of the former patients had been released into the general population. Now it housed the violent and criminally insane, most of them lifers.

Sheldon simply nodded.

"The first order The Institute placed was for winter jackets for all of their patients, all 900 of them. They want them embroidered with patient's names. To fulfill that order, we need a salesperson who isn't afraid to be in that kind of environment. We don't want to screw up the sizes or the names. I'm not gonna sugar-coat it. It could be dangerous. Do you think you could handle such an assignment?"

Sheldon squirmed in his seat.

She noticed his nervousness. "Please, be honest with me, as I believe you have been up to this point. I'm sure you'll have some protection while you're there, but if you don't think you can handle an assignment like that, you have to tell me."

What choice did he have? He was one rent check removed from draining his savings. Then he would be left to max out his credit cards to survive, something he refused to do. "I can handle it."

"You sure?"

"Yes. I'll do it."

"You're hired. Can you start tomorrow?"

"Yes, Mrs. Jacoby."

She stood and offered her hand. "Please, call me Delores. You're part of the team now. Welcome aboard. See you tomorrow morning at eight."

After shaking her hand, surprisingly dry the second time around, he rose and headed to the door.

As he opened it, she said, "And Sheldon?"

He turned around and faced her, his face pale. "Yes, Delores?"

"I don't want you to think I hired you just because you agreed to be our sales rep at The Institute."

"What were the other reasons?"

"I respect your honesty. And I love your black suit."

***

Wrapped securely in a straitjacket, Zach sat in the corner of a white padded room lit by a single light bulb fastened to the ceiling with a thin, dangling cord. Twice a day, Nurse Lenora Ryerson would enter the room, spoon-feed him, and then leave. Hygiene was a little more challenging. Once every three days, four orderlies, a stretcher, ankle and wrist straps, and a rolling trip down those dark and dreary hallways and finally into a shower stall. The whole ordeal would last almost two hours and twice it had been marred by Zach striking out at the orderlies; once with a fist to the face; another time with a single-handed choke hold.

But he was under more powerful and different medication now and hadn't acted out in twenty-eight days. The medication seemed to be working. Zimeon, the black-suited monster, hadn't returned. And Zach had even apologized to Doctor Milo Stanford for mistaking him for the monster. Fortunately the damage he'd inflicted with the mop handle hadn't been life-threatening; a mild concussion and a gash that had required fifteen stitches.

But solitary confinement had been a different story. The loneliness. The isolation. Hell. The first week, horrible hallucinations. A small spider dangling from the light bulb; growing larger, more menacing, then attacking and injecting Zach with its deadly poison and sucking out his entrails, drop by delicious little drop. That hallucination had been followed by bouts of long and agonizing screaming, and finally an intervention by two orderlies, Nurse Ryerson, and an injection of a potent sedative.

During week two, the hallucinations formed a high-resolution and painful replay of Zach's past. Zach was a young boy growing up in a middle-class family with his brother, sister, mother, and father. A loving middle-class family all the way around. But then at fifteen, the voices started. The insidious voices from the pervasive mental malady known as paranoid schizophrenia. The voices told Zach his brother, sister, mother, and father were all just demons in disguise, out to get him and out to kill him and then destroy the world. The worst was his father, who'd started out as loving and caring, at least according to the voices and graphic images. But then he morphed into Zimeon, the black-suited monster, hell-bent on killing and dragging his corpses into the black abyss of hell.

A little play-time and a pack of matches had put an end to Zimeon and his disciples. On a cold winter night, Zach had wandered out to the garage, found a full gas can, and returned to the house. He'd doused the gasoline liberally around the kitchen, produced the long-concealed pack of matches, lit one, dropped it, and presto, problem solved. His mother and father, brother and sister, had burned to death in the ensuing house fire. Demons and devils literally burning in hell. What could be better?

By week three of solitary confinement, a dim yet dreadful realization of what he'd really done forty years ago finally started to jell in Zach's mentally ill mind. He'd committed a heinous atrocity, perpetrated against innocent, loving, and unsuspecting victims. Locked up for all this time, and only now was it beginning to dawn on him on a more visceral and palpable level.

Week four had been punctuated by bouts of depression and sadness, loneliness, and despair, at the grim understanding that he'd inadvertently murdered his entire family. He'd been wracked by sorrow, remorse, and *guilt*—the overriding emotion.

As he thought about it now, he realized that maybe that's why last month Zimeon had begun to haunt and terrorize his sleeping and waking life. It was simple. Zimeon wasn't Zimeon. He was Zach's father Shane, resurrected for the sole purpose of exacting his revenge. His pound of flesh.

Wait a minute. According to Doctor Stanford, who'd forgiven him for the brutal and unprovoked assault, Zimeon wasn't real at all. Zimeon was only a macabre manifestation of Zach's *guilt*. A coping mechanism. A figment of a delusional imagination.

The padded door squeaked open, snapping Zach from his introspection. It brought him back to a semblance of reality—a razor-thin, high-wire act.

Doctor Stanford and Nurse Ryerson entered along with two orderlies. The orderlies carried chairs. They put two chairs next to Zach and left, closing the door behind them. The doctor and nurse sat down.

Producing a pen, Doctor Stanford opened a file and scribbled something. Then he said, "How are we doing today, Zach?"

"I'd like to get outta here, Doc. It's driving me crazy."

Nurse Ryerson, a thin middle-aged woman, concealed a grin with her hand.

"Maybe we can see to that," Doctor Stanford said. "First I'd like to ask you a few questions. Are you up for that?"

Zach would say or do almost anything to get himself out of this hellhole. "Sure."

"Have you seen Zimeon lately?"

"Zimeon isn't real, Doc. You've explained that to me."

"I realize that. I asked you if you've seen him lately."

"No."

"Have you thought about him lately?"

"Only in the context of him being a manifestation of my guilt."

"And how does that make you feel?"

Guilty. Guilty as hell. "Makes me feel like I need to try and control my guilt feelings."

Doctor Stanford scribbled in the file. "Well, as I said, guilt is a powerful, useless, and damaging emotion, one you shouldn't harbor. You weren't responsible for what happened to your family. You had taken leave of your senses."

Criminally insane. Raving lunatic. Nut-job. "I get that, Doc."

"If you continue to harbor guilt there is a danger that Zimeon might return. Do you understand that?"

"Yeah, I'm trying not to harbor any guilt anymore."

"Do you think you're succeeding?"

"Yeah, you've helped me a lot."

"Thank you, Zach. That's what I'm here for. I don't wish to resurrect any monsters, but I am curious about something. The last time we talked, you were evasive about what Zimeon looks like. Since you assaulted me recently, I want to know if he looks like me. I'm here to help you and I don't want you thinking I'm here to hurt you. I don't want you thinking I'm Zimeon. Do you think I'm Zimeon?"

"No."

"What does Zimeon look like?"

A rock and a hard place. To tell the doctor that Zimeon looked like any working stiff wearing a black suit could delay Zach's release. The doctor would probably surmise he couldn't possibly be fit for integration into society if he thought any man or woman wearing a black suit was a monster. Hell, maybe he'd already committed too many unpardonable sins to ever be released, but he couldn't lose hope. That was the one thread he clung to that represented any semblance of sanity. To snip it would mean catatonia and complete lunacy.

"He's"—Zach's black-socket-encircled eyes darted to the floor—"just like the stereotypical images you see of the devil."

"I've seen hundreds of renderings of the devil. What does that mean?"

"He's got an over-sized and red muscular body. He has a big horn-tipped head. He has horse teeth. His face is covered in fur, and he has a nose like a wolf. More like a snout. His eyes are big, round, and red."

The doctor finished scribbling a few notes. "And you don't see him anymore?"

"No."

"You don't think I'm Zimeon anymore?"

"No."

"If I release you into the privacy of your own room, you won't attack me?"

"I'm sorry for that, Doc. I promise I won't attack you again. Please, I beg you, get me outta here."

"You won't attack anyone else on the ward?"

"No. I've apologized to Roger and Phil."

"The two orderlies you attacked?"

"Right. Have they forgiven me?"

"Yes, they have. But they've been assigned to a different area of The Institute for their own protection."

"Sorry about that."

"I accept your apology. They've accepted your apology."

"Okay, good. Does that mean I can leave?"

Doctor Stanford gestured to Nurse Ryerson and she stood, producing a syringe, and squirting a tiny stream of clear liquid into the air.

"If you agree to a sedative, I think it's time to get you out of here. I've never been in favor of the view that solitary confinement rehabilitates patients. If anything, I think it inflames their violent tendencies and makes them even more aggressive. Will you take the needle?"

Zach tried to stretch his arm out but it got constrained by the straitjacket. "Yes, and I'll behave. I promise. Thank you so much, Doc. Thank you so much."

Doctor Stanford pressed a button on a pager clipped to his breast pocket and two orderlies entered the room.

Nurse Ryerson tied off Zach's right leg, found a vein, poked the needle in, and drained the contents.

A pleasant feeling of euphoria swept through Zach as the sedative took effect. He sighed as the orderlies unstrapped the straitjacket.

As he stepped into the hallway, orderlies on each arm, he stopped. His eyes widened in horror and a cold chill shot up his spine. Zimeon, dressed in a black suit and accompanied by hospital administrator Leslie Hopp, was walking right toward him, not thirty feet away. And he was staring right at him. No, looking right through him.

Zach closed his eyes, balled his fists, and gritted his teeth, suppressing the urge to scream by biting down hard on his tongue.

***

Seeing a trickle of blood dribble down the man's chin, Sheldon stopped. He turned to Hopp. "Is he okay?"

Leslie Hopp was a woman in her thirties who looked more like a vengeful district attorney than a hospital administrator, if such a stereotype existed.

When Sheldon had started the tour earlier, an elderly woman with zombie-like eyes and thinning hair had approached him. More like attacked him. Waving a smiling china doll in one hand, she'd muttered something incomprehensible before attempting to smash Sheldon over the head with it. The doll's smiling head had come within a couple of inches of striking Sheldon's unsmiling head.

Hopp hadn't been concerned one iota about Sheldon's safety, replying simply, "Don't worry about Agnes. She's harmless."

Now, however, Hopp stepped aside quickly and pressed her back to the wall. "Over here."

Sheldon quickly joined her, pressing his back tightly against the wall to allow unobstructed passage to the orderlies, the doctor, the nurse, and the patient.

When the patient reached Sheldon, he stopped, suddenly calm and composed. He turned to the doctor. "Hey, Doc, I'd like to meet that man. I'd like to shake his hand."

Doctor Stanford eyed Sheldon briefly, nodded to Hopp politely, and turned to the orderlies. "Release him."

An orderly's eyes widened. "What? He got all tense there. And, look at his lip. He bit it, or bit his tongue. He's bleeding."

Producing a tissue, Nurse Ryerson wiped the smear of blood from Zach's chin. "There, there, you're okay, Zach. Did you bite your tongue?"

"Yeah. I was nervous. So long in solitary. So many people. Made me nervous. I'm fine now."

"Release him," Doctor Stanford said, opening his file and writing something inside it.

The orderlies released Zach.

Sheldon saw something in the man's eyes, a palpable fear mixed with some vague recognition. Something sinister. Something hauntingly familiar. Then it was gone. The man stepped forward and extended his hand. "I'm Zach Middlecoff, and I think I know who you are."

With a steady stream of fear rising in his gut, Sheldon glanced furtively at the medical staff. They each in turn gave him encouraging nods. He tentatively shook the proffered hand. Firm. Dry. Strong. "Sheldon McConnell. Pleased to meet you." *How does he know me?*

Zach released the hand and grinned, wiping a trickle of blood from his lower lip. Gesturing with a waving hand to the others, he made introductions: "These two orderlies are Dean and Reggie. This is Nurse Ryerson and Doctor Stanford, one of the brilliant medical minds here at The Institute."

Smiles and nods, but no handshakes, were exchanged.

Sheldon initially thought better of asking the question, but his morbid curiosity won that battle. To Zach, he asked, "How do you know me?"

"We have a lot in common," Zach said.

We do? You're in a nuthouse. You just got released from solitary confinement. What could we possibly have in common?

It was as if Zach had read Sheldon's mind.

"Yes we do," Zach said. "Something very tragic recently happened to you. And a long time ago, something very tragic happened to me. You recently lost your mother, father, brother, and sister in a tragic house fire. Am I right?"

All the skeletons and demons that Sheldon had thought were securely locked away in a closet sprang to life and began pounding on the incarcerating door and demanding to be released. He fought an urge to turn and run. Run away from The Institute. Run away from the fucking salesman job. Run away from the guilt. Run, run, run, and never stop running until he was certain he'd left all the horror far, far behind.

Instead, he said, "Yeah, you're right. Did that happen to you?"

Zach's eyes glazed over. "Yes, unfortunately, it did. I lost my family in a tragic house fire."

"That's incredible," Doctor Stanford said. "Incredible that Zach would know that."

"Thank you, Doc," Zach said. "I know a lot more about him. I might even know more than he knows."

"You do?" Sheldon said. *Run, run, run.*

"I know you've been wracked by guilt for a long time," Zach said. "And so was I. But Doctor Stanford, a miracle worker, showed me the light."

"He did?" It was all Sheldon could think of to say.

Zach nodded knowingly. "Yes, he did. He taught me that guilt is a powerful, useless, and damaging emotion, one you shouldn't harbor. You weren't responsible for what happened to your family. You had taken leave of your senses."

Doctor Stanford's eyes widened as he jotted something in the file.

In spite of his nervousness, fear, and shock at meeting a patient at The Institute who'd practically gone through the same tragic ordeal he had, Sheldon realized there was probably one big difference. He hadn't started the fire that had killed his parents. Faulty wiring had done that. Zach, on the other hand, was locked up in a mental asylum for the criminally insane. That could only mean one thing. He'd started the fire that had killed his family. He'd murdered his family. *That nut-job roasted his family extra crispy over a house-sized, open-flame barbeque.* The thought made him angry. Who did this crazy person think he was? Accusing Sheldon of murdering his family in a moment of insanity? Nothing could be further from the truth.

"The difference between us," Sheldon said, feeling his cheeks redden, "is you murdered your parents and faulty wiring killed mine."

"Are you sure about that?" Zach asked matter-of-factly. "Are you sure you didn't get a little gas and douse the house, trying to kill the demons? Trying to kill Zimeon and his minions."

Sheldon clenched his teeth. Zimeon? *Who the fuck is Zimeon? This fuck is trying to transfer his guilt to me. I'll be fucked if I'm gonna let that happen.* "I don't know what you're talking about. I wasn't even home when that fire started. I didn't even live there at the time."

"And you're sure about that?" Zach said. "You're sure you didn't dig out that box of matches you'd kept hidden for just the right moment? Then strike a match, drop it on the gas, and, presto, problem solved."

Sheldon clenched his fist and stepped forward before realizing it. But he stopped himself at the last second. *Words are mightier than the sword, or in this case, a knuckle sandwich.* "I know what you're doing and I won't take the bait. You're transferring your guilt to me or trying to anyway. If you can't come to grips with the fact that you're a murderer, that's not my problem."

Doctor Stanford stepped in the middle of the two combatants. "All right, boys. I think this has gone far enough."

"Fucking right it has," Sheldon said, now seething. He unhooked the plastic visitor badge pinned to his chest and thrust it down hard on the floor, shattering it into a million pieces. "I didn't sign up for this bullshit. No job in the world is worth being accused of murder by some fucking nutcase."

His eyes roamed quickly over the faces of the staff, all of whom were looking at him incredulously. His gaze stopped at Zach and he fixed him with a cold stare. "Blaming someone else for your sins isn't going to absolve you of them. Remember that, you fucking nut-case."

Zach gave him a shit-eating grin. "Come to terms with your guilt and everything will be okay. Zimeon is a manifestation of your guilt. To get rid of him you have to get rid of your guilt."

"Fuck you," Sheldon said, turning to hospital administrator Leslie Hopp. "Don't worry, I'll let myself out. Thanks for your fake fucking protection."

"Wait," she said. "Everything's gonna be all right."

Sheldon was already halfway down the hall, almost at a full sprint. He came to an abrupt stop when he saw a glowing red neon EMERGENCY EXIT sign. Before pushing open the door, he looked back.

The two orderlies, Dean and Reggie, were coming after him.

***

Sheldon woke up dizzy and sleepy the following morning with the initial impression that yesterday had been nothing more than a terrible nightmare. But the room told a different story. White padded walls. No windows. A bedside table and two chairs. A single lightbulb dangling from the middle of the ceiling. A small steel desk and chair off to the side. A door in the corner of the room marked BATHROOM.

"What the fuck," he said, struggling to move his arms. But they wouldn't move. He noticed they were bound to the steel headboard by steel and leather wrist straps. He struggled to move his legs. Same thing. Ankle bracelets, not of the decorative kind.

Panic and raw fear shot through him like a lightning bolt. "Hey, get me out of here! There's been a mistake! Somebody, get me out of here! Pleeeeeeeeeease, let me go!!!"

The white padded door squeaked open and Nurse Ryerson and Doctor Stanford entered. They sat down next to the bed.

"What's going on?" Sheldon asked. "What am I doing here? There's been a mistake. Let me go. Please!" Sheldon felt his eyes moisten as a wave of depression, sadness, and helplessness cascaded over him. He wanted to wipe the tears away, but he couldn't move.

Nurse Ryerson stepped up to the plate, pulling out a tissue and wiping his eyes before sitting down. "There, there. Everything's gonna be just fine."

He was about to start a profanity-laden rant but bit his tongue so hard he drew blood. He swallowed the coppery-tasting liquid, unwilling to tip his hand to his two captors. *Go along with them. Stay calm and they'll let you go. They have to. You don't belong here.*

Doctor Stanford opened his file and reviewed some notes. His eyes left the file and found Sheldon. "How are you feeling?"

"I'm fine, Doc. There's been a mistake. I shouldn't be here. I have work to do. I need to go."

"We'll get to that in a minute. Do you remember what happened yesterday?"

"Yeah. Clear as day. I came here as a sales representative on behalf of Jacoby Style & Sportswear to take the winter jacket order for your patients. One of your patients freaked me out and I ran."

"Do you remember the name of the patient who upset you?"

"Zach. Zach Middlecoff."

"And what's your name?"

"Sheldon. Sheldon McConnell."

After a long pause during which he scratched his chin and adjusted his low-hanging bifocals, Doctor Stanford crinkled his brow and studied Sheldon. "It seems I miscalculated your progress. I thought we were doing so well, but it appears now you've had a bit of a relapse. I can only hope that there is some upside in this relapse."

Play along, play along, play along. "What do you mean, Doc?"

"Your name is not Sheldon McConnell. You're Zach Middlecoff."

"What? No."

"I'm afraid so, Zach. I think you invented this other personality, this Sheldon, as a way to deal with your guilt. The same way you invented Zimeon. Don't you see, Sheldon arrived to help you cope? First, he was a monster, this Zimeon, and then you transformed him into Sheldon as you started to work through your guilt. After we captured and sedated you yesterday, Zach returned and Zach described Sheldon as wearing a black suit. Zach also described Zimeon as wearing a black suit. Maybe something positive will come out of all of this. It gives me some hope that at first Zach viewed Zimeon as a monster and now Zach views Zimeon as Sheldon, a guilt-ridden and troubled man, yet a friendly man who Zach wants not only to meet but to help come to terms with his guilt."

The whole analysis was too overwhelming and confusing to Sheldon. He bit his tongue hard a second time and swallowed a trickle of blood. *Play along, play along, play along. He said something positive will emerge.* "So, maybe I am getting better."

"Perhaps. You still have a long way to go but it's encouraging for me to see that Zimeon the monster has been replaced by Sheldon, the troubled and guilt-ridden man struggling to come to terms with his tragic past."

"But I'm Sheldon."

"You are now. That'll change soon I suspect."

Sheldon felt his heart rate quicken, veins in his neck beginning to pulse and throb. He was about to bite down a third time on his tongue but the taste of his own blood was already making him queasy.

So, instead, he just screamed bloody murder.

Nurse Ryerson quickly produced a chloroform-soaked white cloth and smothered Sheldon's screaming mouth with it. In a few seconds he closed his mouth, closed his eyes, and passed out.

"Nice work," Doctor Stanford said. "Inject the sedative now. We need to keep him down for a while. It will take some time before he comes to grips with his multiple personalities, never mind the therapeutic benefits of them."

***

As was her talent, hospital administrator Leslie Hopp was busy in her office multi-tasking when one of the phone lines flashed red.

Good, she thought, eager to cut the janitorial supply salesman off the line. Too aggressive for her tastes. "Sorry, Jeremy, gonna have to call you back. An important meeting to attend." Of course, there was no important meeting. The line was just part of her bunburying tactics.

Hopp pressed the flashing red button and the speaker squawked static for a split-second before her secretary said, "There's a call on line three for you, Ms. Hopp."

"Who is it?"

"A salesman."

Not again. It was high time The Institute hired a purchasing agent. She hated dealing with sales reps. "Take a message and tell him I'm in a meeting." But some strange and mysterious feeling prompted her to ask, "What's his name?"

The speaker squawked static again, prompting Hopp to cover her ears with her hands in annoyance.

When the static cleared, her secretary said, "Sheldon. Sheldon Middlecoff."

Where's My Money?

Belinda Methusda was obsessed with money for one simple reason. As a child, she never had any. She'd grown up in Brantford, Ontario, in the early 60s, the only child of two parents, Martha and Stan, who'd lived through the Great Depression before emigrating from England to Canada. That experience had drilled into their DNA the "Waste not, want not" philosophy, and the starvation and daily struggles of that era had also infected them with a Scarcity Mentality, which they'd, in turn, passed on to their daughter.

When Belinda grew into an adult, the Scarcity Mentality manifested itself in many ways. Her view of life was that there was only so much wealth available, not an abundance of it. Only one pie and the bigger other people's slices got, the smaller hers' became. So she'd made it her life's mission to get the biggest slice possible, even though in her parochial view of life, that amounted to smaller portions for others. The notion of more than one pie simply never crossed her mind.

Belinda's Scarcity Mentality also made her very stingy with the few friends she had, unwilling to share a drink, a meal, or, heaven forbid, a dollar with them.

Where it manifested itself the most pronounced and the most damaging was in the work place. As an accountant rising to the top of a large accounting firm, Belinda refused to share credit and recognition, power or profit, with any of her colleagues; even those who may have inspired or helped her with cost-cutting proposals or business-savvy marketing tips.

It was all about her. It was all about her rise to the top. And, no, there just wasn't enough to go around, so don't bother asking.

She opened the door to her bare-bones condo in Toronto's skyline, kicked off her shoes on the inside mat, flicked on a hall light, and walked into the living room, setting her briefcase down and heading straight for the kitchen. She brushed back a lock of her frilly black hair, opened the fridge, and grabbed a plastic container containing her latest cooking concoction—ground beef with macaroni and cheese, onions, and a few spices. She'd eaten the same bland meal for the last three days, even though she was on the verge of becoming a full partner in Matheson, Brand & Humphrey, a position which would quadruple her income and provide lucrative profit-sharing in the firm. Never mind the looming promotion, she'd already skimped and saved her entire 59 years, carried no debt, owned her condo clear-title, and had socked away nearly a million dollars in low-risk, income-producing investments.

Waste not, want not. But she paused as she dished the food into a plate and prepared to put it into the microwave. *You can afford better. No, I can't. Not now. When I get the promotion. That's when I'll treat myself.*

Satisfied with that justification, she pressed a button on the microwave, poured herself a glass of no-name concentrated orange juice, and sat down at the tiny kitchen island, running some numbers in her head for her latest money-saving proposal—a clever, albeit dishonest scheme to include coffee breaks and lunch breaks as billable hours.

Just as the microwave beeped news that her hot and delicious dinner was ready to devour, her cell phone rang. She noticed it was her mother and wrestled with the notion of answering it. She hadn't spoken to Martha in about three months. Lately, she hadn't liked what was coming out of her mother's mouth. She, of all people, telling Belinda to try and enjoy some of her money instead of being so tight-fisted. But despite her reluctance, she answered the call.

When the preliminary niceties were dispensed with, Martha said, "I'm worried about you."

"Really? What's there to be worried about? I'm on the cusp of a big promotion that will make me a full partner in the firm."

"That's great news, Belinda, but that's exactly what I'm worried about."

"My promotion? You must be kidding me, Mom. You don't think I'll get it?"

"No, quite the contrary. I think you'll get it and it won't change anything. You keep telling me that when you reach a certain milestone financially, you'll start treating yourself, start sharing with others. I'm afraid that milestone will never come."

How dare she? "Wait a second. You and Dad were the ones who taught me the value of a buck. You guys instilled in me the philosophy of Waste not, want not. I'm a product of your upbringing and now you're telling me it's all wrong?"

A long and uncomfortable pause.

Finally, she replied, "I just want you to treat yourself once in a while. Go on a date. Go see a movie. Go out for dinner. When was the last time you took a vacation?"

Even though Belinda was becoming agitated, she had to admit she honestly couldn't remember the last time she'd taken a vacation. Fifteen years at the accounting form and no vacation. Was that the truth? Was she that scared to part with her money, fearing it would lead to a free-spending frenzy that would spiral her into financial ruin? What about a date? Had her fears that a man would take her money prevented her from engaging with the opposite sex? Unless she counted the time many years ago when she had lost her virginity to her high school sweetheart. Had it really been that long ago? She didn't want to admit the answer. She felt the walls that she'd so intricately constructed—aided and abetted by her parents—begin to close in around her.

She decided a lie would have to suffice. For now. "As soon as I get the promotion, I'm taking a trip to Cuba. For a whole month."

"I hope you do. I really hope you do. You told me when you reached middle-management you'd treat yourself to a vacation and what did you do?"

Belinda was drawing a blank. Because that's all there was. Yet she remained defensive. "That was different, Mom. I was just clawing my way to the top back then."

"Listen, honey, I've heard it all before. Because I invented it. I invented all kinds of reasons why I couldn't have what I wanted. Why I couldn't buy my less fortunate friends the occasional lunch. Why I couldn't give to the needy. Why I couldn't buy that new dress. Why I couldn't buy that new appliance. I was the master of deceit—my own self-deceit and self-deception."

Belinda was on the verge of tears and her voice cracked with emotion. "What happened to you? You used to be so proud of my spend-thrift ways. You used to praise my saving habits. My living frugally. My ability to not over-indulge. My talent with money. You brought me up this way."

The emotion in her mother's voice was unmistakable. "What happened to me is I got old, and wise. I'm 92 now and can barely get out of bed in the morning. My whole body aches with arthritis. Your father isn't doing much better. Sure, I taught you some good ways. But it took me this long to realize that I was also misguided, in many ways a victim of my own upbringing. I should've also taught you to enjoy your life because life is short and then you die. I'm so sorry I didn't tell you earlier. I'm so sorry for my part in who you are now. But, I'm telling you now, I'm begging you now, go out and enjoy your life before it's too late."

"I'll take that trip, Mom. I promise."

"I hope so, for your sake. And remember, it's not all about giving to yourself. It's also about giving to others and helping others. It's true that the greater joy comes with giving. Not with receiving."

Belinda was becoming overwhelmed with emotion and was beginning to fear she would blurt out something offensive. "Mom, I appreciate this. My dinner's going cold. Can I eat now?"

"Of course you can. And come and visit us some time. We haven't seen you in months. Enjoy your dinner."

Belinda looked at the last vestiges of steam rising from her mac-and-cheese concoction and suddenly lost her appetite. "Bye, Mom. Say hi to Dad."

***

"Where's my money?"

The voice behind the question sounded odd to Belinda.

"Where's my money?"

Hearing it the second time, she cringed as she realized it was her voice. She'd left her apartment for the day. Where she'd gone wasn't abundantly clear. However, upon returning home, she noticed a number of things missing. In a panic, she rummaged around the entire suite, finally locating her purse containing credit cards and important identification. Why she hadn't brought the purse with her was a mystery. Overriding that mystery was her sense of dread and loss at the missing money. She usually kept a few hundred dollars—in this case exactly $364.23—inside the purse.

And it was nowhere to be found.

Carrying the purse, she left the bedroom and went into the living room. Four people sat huddled around her coffee table playing cards, plumes of cigarette smoke twirling up and forming a blue hazy cloud above the uninvited guests.

She stopped in front of them, consternation etching her brow. "Where's my money?"

A long-haired, freaky-looking guy exhaled a plume of smoke toward her. "What money, honey?"

The other three long-haired, freaky-looking guys burst into laughter. One said, "I like that. 'What money, honey?' Maybe you ask nicely, maybe we give it to you. How 'bout, 'Where's my money, honey?'"

Hysterical laughter filled the room.

When it subsided, Belinda said, "You can't smoke in here. You can't be in here."

"You can't stop us," one said.

"I'll call the police."

"You don't have a phone," another said.

Belinda's face tightened and she rummaged through her purse looking for the phone. Not there. She returned to the bedroom and scoured it thoroughly but came up empty-handed. Then she remembered her secret stash of cash and wondered if the intruders had found it. She removed a framed picture of a garishly elongated CN Tower from the wall and flipped it around. She sighed. Taped to the back was an envelope, which she knew contained five thousand in cash, her emergency stash. She removed the envelope. Its bulk felt right. She quickly tore it open and peered inside.

"What?"

The hundred dollar bills had been replaced with currency-sized blank pieces of paper.

In the unlikely event she was seeing things, she stuffed the envelope into her purse and stormed out into the living room. "Where's my emergency cash-stash?"

"What money, honey?" one man said.

"If there's more, hand it over," another said. "I'm losing big-time."

More riotous laughter.

This can't be real. Can't be real. Yet it felt so real. "That's it, I'm fetching the police." Belinda rushed out the door in the hope that one of two things would happen. She'd be able to flag down someone and recruit their help to call the police. Or, she'd return to her apartment a few minutes later and everything would be back to normal. She'd wake from this crazy nightmare and resume her normal routine. She moved quickly down the dimly lit and people-less hallway. In her rising panic, it never occurred to her to knock on doors.

Outside, the streets were abandoned. Not a single car. Not a single light. Only an eerie blue-gray mist enveloping the city. She cried out to the emptiness: "WHERE'S MY MONEY!"

Her voice echoed back hollowly.

She roamed in every direction. But still she found no sign of life. She was in an eerie post-apocalyptic landscape. She thought grimly that even if she did find her money, it probably wouldn't help her now.

But the financial loss was still deeply troubling. The more she walked, the angrier she got. She stopped and spun around, wondering if she had gone too far and would no longer be able to locate her low-rise apartment building. But there it was, closer than ever and illuminated by a glowing lightbulb above the entrance. With renewed purpose she marched home, entered, and practically flew up the three flights of stairs to the number that marked her unit.

Balling her fists, she rehearsed her lines briefly in her head and then opened the door and stepped inside, slamming it behind her.

"GIVE ME MY MONEY BACK AND GET THE FUCK OUTTA HERE!"

But the room was empty. She was back in her bedroom, sitting bolt-upright in bed, sweating profusely, shoulders heaving, looking at four plain walls, one of which contained the CN Tower picture, no longer garishly elongated.

She breathed a long sigh and checked the time. 7:23 am. Time to get ready for work.

***

It was nearing the end of the day and she'd been nervous and fidgety for most of it. In part due to the horrific nightmare, which, to her credit, she had gone some way to dismissing as nothing more than an anomalous event triggered by her mother's bad advice and deconstructive criticism. Whatever you wanted to call it, the lecture had been unhelpful and hurtful, especially since Belinda was merely a product of everything her mother had staunchly espoused to her while she was growing up. To assuage her fears after waking from that terrible nightmare, Belinda had even gone so far as to count her emergency cash-stash and purse money to the penny.

Fortunately everything had added up.

Belinda's nervousness was mainly about the promotion. Her mother had planted seeds of doubt that had taken root and begun sprouting as toxic weeds of despair and uncertainty.

Today was supposed to be the day of the big announcement and she thought she would've heard from senior partner Lorena Matheson by now regarding the promotion. Yet nothing so far. And here it was Friday, 4:50 pm, ten minutes away from quitting time. Not for Belinda, though, since she had her own key and frequently put in longer hours than her colleagues, trying to score brownie points in anticipation of the promotion.

As she put away the plastic container that still held remnants of her mac-and-cheese dinner, microwaved and eaten at her desk during lunch, a light on her desk phone brightened and buzzed, yanking her out of her reverie.

Sitting in front of Lorena Matheson, Belinda clasped her hands together, placing them on one crossed knee, trying to conceal their clamminess. She leaned forward in her chair and looked at Lorena, waiting for her to remove her eyes from the file she'd been reading, a proposal by Belinda to ditch the high-rise office space the firm rented and buy a commercial office building on the outskirts of the inner-city core. Belinda had analyzed the numbers to the nth degree and buying as opposed to leasing definitely made financial sense. With the building Belinda had located, the firm could virtually cover the financing on the building with other tenant leases and, at least on paper, show a modest positive cash flow. Not to mention the firm would be building real estate equity instead of throwing money out the window, only to be snapped up by the grubby hands of greedy landlords.

Lorena adjusted her bifocals, closed the file, and looked at Belinda. "I see you've really done your research on this building acquisition. And all on your own time. Impressive. I love the idea. Not only that, I'd like to charge you personally with overseeing the acquisition."

"Thank you," Belinda said, hardly able to contain her giddiness. She was glad she'd submitted the building acquisition proposal in favor of one calling for billing clients for staff lunch breaks and coffee breaks. That scheme was a little, if not a lot, dishonest. She'd have to sharpen her pencil a little to provide it with an air of legitimacy.

"You can start working on the building acquisition tomorrow. Or tonight, if that is your want."

"I'll get right on it," Belinda said. "But I thought acquisitions was Earl Brand's department?" Brand was one of the other partners; however, there were rumors circulating that he was about to be bought out, was close to retirement, or had decided to leave the firm and branch out on his own. Belinda hadn't heard which one, or two, of them might be true.

"Brand has decided to retire," Lorena said, folding her hands together. "And we'd like to offer you a full partnership in the firm."

Beaming, Belinda stood and extended her hand. "Thank you so much, Mrs. Matheson. I'd love to be a full partner."

Lorena stood, stepped around her desk, and gave Belinda a warm hug. "You're welcome, and welcome aboard. And you can call me Lorena now. We're family."

After Lorena had explained some of the perks and responsibilities of being a partner at Matheson, Brand & Humphrey, Belinda got up to leave.

"One more thing," Lorena said.

Belinda spun around on feet that were as light as feathers. "What's that, Lorena?"

"Try and have some fun in your life once in a while. There's more to life than work. All work and no play makes Belinda a dull girl."

***

Belinda stood outside of her apartment door, her purse in one hand, a bottle of red wine in the other. For the very first time in her life, she'd decided to reward herself for her accomplishments and actually bought herself a little celebratory gift on her way home. And she had to admit, it felt good. She couldn't wait to have a drink and celebrate her good fortune. Maybe she would even call her mother and tell her the good news. And make a point of mentioning the celebratory gift.

She hoped her newfound willingness to indulge herself a little wasn't fleeting. She hoped it wasn't too late to begin to lead a more fulfilling life. *No, definitely not a case of too little, too late.*

She opened her purse and fished around for her apartment key. She froze when she thought she heard a murmur from the other side of the door.

Then she heard it, loud and clear: "Where's my money, honey?"

"Don't be ridiculous," she said after a moment of shocked hesitation, her elation trouncing on the split-second of fear and obliterating it.

She was just about to insert her apartment key into the keyhole when something else occurred to her. The little change purse containing $364.23. Where was it? She should have at least palmed it or touched it by now.

Beginning to tremble, she kneeled down, put down the bottle of wine and her keys, and rummaged through her purse. Nothing. *No money, honey.*

"Where's my money?"

Fractured Skull

"Sometimes it feels like it never ends," Dawson Shallihan said.

John Pickett removed his baseball cap, wiped a sweaty brow, and studied the long and winding road. "What do you mean? It's only a mile long. It has to end."

Dawson knew a few things about the road that John didn't. Sure it lead to the beach, his beach, on Prince Edward Island, where he'd painstakingly cleared an old road and an old site that had been grandfathered in. He'd heard the stories about its history from a man who'd married one of the daughters of the old household long before he'd come along and bought the property for a song. Blaine Saunders had said the road held many mysteries, most of them related to moonshine production and distribution during the era of Prohibition.

Dawson remembered well the last conversation he'd had with Blaine, before his mysterious and untimely death.

"One time we took a load of moonshine down to the water and began loading it on one of our customer's boats," Blaine had said. "But shit hit the fan. Those assholes starting complaining that the order wasn't right. Tried to accuse us of shorting them. We'd never do that. You can imagine what happened after that."

"I have no idea," Dawson had said.

"The guns came out. Shots were fired."

Of course that begged several questions. Questions that, since Dawson now owned the 30 acres of waterfront property, he didn't want to know the answers to. *Was anyone killed? Where were they buried? Were you shot? Did you kill anybody?*

Was anybody charged? The list went on and on, but Dawson hadn't pressed the matter. Instead he'd plied Blaine with a few shots from a bottle of moonshine he'd found buried on the property, still remarkably preserved, and gently steered the conversation to other more mundane topics.

"Are you daydreaming?" John said. "I said the road has to end."

Dawson rubbed his eyes, hoping that eventually his memory of the moonshine stories would fade, and turned to John. Should he let dead dogs lie? Some of them, maybe. But not all of them. *Ah, fuck it.* "I mean sometimes when I drive it, it seems to take me a lot longer than other times. Especially at night."

"That's easy to explain," John said. "You can't see shit at night. All the little bends that you're normally familiar with become obscured and you don't know shit from Shinola."

Dawson picked up his chainsaw and put it on the tailgate of his pickup. It had run out of gas and the chain needed tightening. Since John, a transplant to the Island three years ago, had volunteered to help him cut his way through storm-downed trees to the beach, he began to wonder about the wisdom of potentially scaring him off. The job they were doing was dangerous enough without throwing gas on the fire. Why couldn't he just leave it alone? Because John was a Doubting Thomas that's why. And he needed to be taught a lesson in respect. Respect for Mother Nature. Respect for the dead. Dawson didn't have to be told. He knew on a gut level people had been killed at his beachfront and buried in his back thirty. The question was where were they? Would they disentomb skulls and bones this fall Saturday afternoon while chain-sawing? Dawson shuddered, tightening the gas cap on the chainsaw after refilling it. He flipped the saw on its side and began to work the chain-tightening nuts loose while John ran a gloved hand over the chain on his chainsaw, checking its tautness.

"How do you explain it happening in the daytime as well?" Dawson asked.

John grinned, buck-toothed. "I'd call that some pretty potent hooch. Or maybe some pretty potent weed. Or maybe both."

"It's happened when I was sober."

"In your imagination maybe. I've been down your road several times. It has a clear beginning, middle, and end. Period."

Frowning, Dawson finished tightening the chain. John had left little, if any, room for discussion. Maybe he *should* just let it go. Free labor was free labor. Period. "I guess you're right. Just my mind playing tricks on me. Let's get to work."

John grinned and fired up his chainsaw. They went to work, methodically cutting their way to the beach. They would cut down a tree blocking the road, buck the firewood, and stack it neatly at the road side. Then they would toss the limbs—logging slash—in out-of-the-way and less forested locations, trying to minimize their footprint. An hour and six trees later they reached what Dawson recognized as the halfway point and they stopped for a break. Dawson retrieved two cans of beans from a small cooler in the truck, two bottles of water, a can opener, and two tablespoons. He sat on the tailgate next to John and offered him a can of beans and a bottle of water, which John eagerly accepted.

"It's nothing fancy," Dawson said. "But it hits the spot in a pinch."

As they ate, John said, "Hey, when's this road end?"

Dawson couldn't tell from his tone, even and without emotion, whether he was being sarcastic or not. He thought he'd play it safe, at least until after they'd worked their way to the beach. He didn't want to lose his volunteer labor now. He knew only too well the potential dangers of logging alone.

He pointed to a bend about fifty feet in front of the truck. It was blocked by a large fallen spruce tree. "That there is about the halfway point. After that, the road forks and we can cut through the path of least resistance. I can leave the other side until another time if you want."

John stuffed a spoonful of cold beans into his mouth. "We'll see how our energy goes. I don't mind helping you. And, who knows, maybe it'll be clear sailing after that bend."

"I hope so. Thanks for your help. I really appreciate it."

"Just put it on my bill."

"I owe you. Let's put it that way."

"The price will be high."

"How about a case of beer? Plus I'll help you load your winter wood."

"Sure, I'll take the case of beer, and the help with the wood. But I'm not really worried about it. We're neighbors. Neighbors help each other."

Between spoonfuls of beans, Dawson studied his friend. When John had first bought the home on ten acres next door, Dawson had been suspicious of him—a transplant from the big city of Toronto. Dawson had his doubts the clean-cut, bookish-looking character would be able to adapt to country life. A retired ad executive. Yeah, right. Dawson, on the other hand, had grown up on the Island, always doing manual labor—fishing, farming, logging, all physically demanding. He'd asked for and received a chainsaw for his thirteenth birthday.

Their friendship was odd to say the least. Dawson, a grizzled, giant of a man, and John, a diminutive converted city slicker. But John had surprised Dawson. Small but strong. A quick study with the chainsaw, an even quicker study with construction and land clearing. It was as if he'd been suppressing his survivalist genes for so many years. And now that they were out of the closet, they were rapidly transforming him into a rough-edged and resourceful rural red neck. He'd even begun growing his hair out, sporting chin scruff, and dumbing down his vocabulary, often peppering his comments with colorful profanity.

"You've turned into a good neighbor," Dawson said. "And you're starting to look more like an Islander every day. What's with the chin scruff? And that little shadow on your upper lip?"

"It's my attempt at a goatee. I'll never be able to grow a beard like you, but what do you think?"

"It might fill out. I never liked the clean-cut accountant image. I think it's an improvement."

"Well, I'm not in the big-city corporate world anymore, am I? Other than Doris, I don't have too many people to please. And she's gone totally country bumpkin, so she doesn't care. Actually she encouraged me to grow my hair out and grow some peach fuzz. Can you fucking believe it? She used to be the model of fashion in the city, and now she looks like a Tom-boy."

"But you like it?"

"I might not have before, but, yeah, I do now. Hey, what if we get beyond that bend and we don't see the fork?"

"Now I know you're fucking with me. I wasn't sure earlier."

John scratched his patchy growth and frowned. "Actually, I'm not fucking with you. The reason I was so curious before is because when you said sometimes the road feels never-ending a strange feeling came over me."

"What do you mean? You were shooting down my story."

"It was my own shit, Dawson. I had a nightmare last night that I was driving on a long and winding country road that wouldn't end. It was creepy. I woke up covered in sweat and terrified. By lunch time, I was looking at the dream as a metaphor for my corporate life and I started to feel better. Because, I'm out of it now. In the country and not cow-towing to the demands of corporate culture. But when you mentioned the never-ending road, I started to think that I just replaced one caged rat exercise wheel for another one. Same shit, different pile, but still going round and round. So I got defensive and tried to downplay it."

Dawson wondered if he should tell John about the moonshine story and his theory about how it might relate to the long road home. No, they had work to do. Better leave it for another day. Get to the beach. Get back home safely.

"Now you're freaking me out," Dawson said. "Can we get this done, and talk about it over a few beers?"

John's smile returned as he tossed his empty bean can into the pickup bed. "Let's fucking get 'er done, man."

When they arrived at the downed spruce, Dawson was relieved to see the fork in the distance. The left side looked unobstructed and the right was clogged with at least six storm-damaged trees.

Dawson pointed. "There you go. The fork. This road's not never-ending. Four hundred or so feet past the fork is the water's edge."

Before firing up the chainsaws to clear the tree in front of them, they discussed their approach to the beach. They decided to take the clear left fork to the water, assess the beach area damage, and circle back around and tackle the obstructed fork from behind on their return trip to Dawson's house.

It took less than fifteen minutes to make quick work of the seventy-foot, eighteen-inch-diameter spruce tree. They returned their chainsaws to the pickup and drove the remaining four hundred feet to the water's edge. There they surveyed the damage. There were a half a dozen or so storm-downed trees at the water's edge, a few others on the perimeter of the clearing, but none that posed a threat to their return trip to the house. And today's goal after all was to cut their way to the beach. They'd done that, and as they admired the bright red, orange, and yellow fall colors and the expansive view out to sea, Dawson wondered if enough was enough. They could easily drive the one-mile road home and call it a day, tackling the right fork another day. It was also going on five pm and the sun would be setting in another two hours. After hearing John's nightmare, he certainly didn't want to be operating a chainsaw on at dusk.

"Why don't we wrap it up?" Dawson asked.

"Let's do the right fork. We made it this far. You're not getting tired, are you?"

That decided it. Never show weakness. Especially not to a city-slicker-turned-country-boy. "Let's get 'er fucking done then."

"That's the spirit. Let's go, Rocko."

"Rocko?"

"It just popped into my head."

They went to work on the right fork. John used a small chainsaw to limb branches and Dawson used a bigger chainsaw to cut through the downed trees, some as large as two feet in diameter. Cutting some smaller trees snagged under a larger tree, Dawson was careful to pay attention to the angle of tension in the timber, so as not to have any trees snap back in their faces. On one small maple, he misjudged the angle and the tree snapped back at them. Dawson saw it coming and leaped out of the way just in time, but John wasn't so lucky. His head was down, focusing on limbing branches while standing about six feet behind Dawson. The maple snapped off with a loud crack, shot toward his head like a spear, and clipped him in the side of the head. His baseball cap flew off, he dropped his chainsaw, and dropped to the ground, yelling, "Oh fuck, Oh fuck, Oh fuck... "

Dawson killed his chainsaw, set it down, rushed over, and bent down to John. There was a small cut above his right ear that was dribbling blood down the side of his face. A goose egg was beginning to sprout.

"Are you okay?" Dawson said. "Shit, you're bleeding. I should've had you stand farther back."

John staggered to his feet and Dawson helped him over to a large stump and sat him down. He quickly found John's abandoned chainsaw, turned it off, and returned to his friend. John's eyes were swimming in circles.

"You okay?" Dawson asked again.

"Yeah, I'm dizzy. Gimme a minute. My head will clear."

Dawson went to his pickup, opened the glove box, and pulled out a first-aid kit. He returned to John, opened the kit, and removed and opened a rubbing-alcohol swab. He used it to clean up John's cut, opened a few more, and used them to wipe most of the blood from the side of John's face. He then produced a tube of topical antibiotic cream, dabbed the wound liberally, and then bandaged it with a one-by-three inch adhesive bandage. John's eyes looked dizzily at the darkening sky during the entire process.

"The cut doesn't look that deep," Dawson said. "But I don't like the look of that growing lump. Let's go home."

John's eyes slowly found focus. "Thanks. My head's starting to clear."

"Sorry about that," Dawson said. "I misjudged the angle of compression."

John grinned. "Don't worry about it. Shit happens. I shouldn't have been so close to you. You know the professionals don't advise logging that close together."

"I know. It was stupid on my part."

"Don't take the blame. I should've known. I do know."

Dawson gathered up the chainsaws and loaded them into the pickup. Then he collected the plastic bin containing gas and oil and chainsaw tools and placed it in the truck.

"No. Let's finish this," John said. "Two more trees to go, then we can drive straight through. Otherwise we gotta backtrack a few hundred feet."

Dawson scratched his head. John had a point. Already the road was darkening behind them, the sun beginning to set up ahead, providing slightly better visibility. "I'll do it, then. You stay put and rest."

John gave the thumbs up and Dawson went to work. Soon he had both trees unsnagged, dropped, and cut up. He killed the chainsaw and smiled broadly.

"All set," Dawson said.

"Way to go."

"We did it." Dawson approached John, gave him a high-five, and then went to work stacking firewood and piling tree branches. John got to his feet unsteadily and began helping him.

When they were finished, another high five had them both heading toward the truck. Dawson felt something strange—bone-snapping strange—crunch underfoot and a chill shot up his spine, standing the hairs on his back to full attention.

He stopped and looked down. The hollow eye of a caved-in skull stared up at him. "Oh, fuck."

"What?" John said. He closed the passenger door of the truck and went around to where Dawson was standing, his foot frozen to the skull. "Holy shit. Is that what I think it is?"

"Yeah," Dawson said. "Get a flashlight. In the glovebox."

While John retrieved a flashlight, Dawson slowly removed his foot. From what he could see, it looked like his steel-shanked logging boot had caved in the right side of the skull. Bone fragments dotted the perimeter of the skull forming the shape of a toe. Dawson's toe. Dawson's boot.

"Where do you think it came from?" John asked, kneeling down with a lit flashlight and examining it closely.

"Before my time, this road used to be used for moonshine distribution," Dawson said. "They used to bring orders to the waterfront and load them onto boats."

"Holy shit," John said. "I knew there was a lot of moonshine production around these parts, but I didn't realize your property was one of them."

Dawson got right to the point. "One of the former residents of this property told me that a gunfight broke out during one of the deliveries. I don't know all the details. I didn't ask."

"I get it," John said. "I wouldn't either. Maybe this unlucky guy was one of the casualties."

"That's what I'm thinking."

"What should we do with the skull?"

Dawson's mind raced. *What do you do with a skull that you find on your property? Call the cops? Bury it deeper and keep your mouth shut?* An answer didn't immediately come to him. He did know he certainly wasn't gonna spend what little remained of the dim light of dusk exhuming skeletal remains. *What was beneath it? The rest of the body?*

"I need to think this over," Dawson said. "I think it's time to go."

John offered no protest. He rubbed his bandaged head and turned toward the truck. He staggered slightly and Dawson leaped forward and grabbed his arm, steadying him.

"Thanks," John said. "Sudden wave of dizziness."

Dawson helped him into the passenger seat, set his chainsaw in the truck bed, walked around to the driver side and stopped, taking one last look at the hollow eyes peering up at him from the shallow grave. Black holes that held a mystery. For a split second, the thought he saw one of the eyes blink and almost jumped out of his skin. No, he quickly reassured himself. Twilight playing tricks on his mind. Nothing more. But nonetheless, he was thankful the skull was behind the truck and not in front of it. He would hate like hell to have to drive over it on the way home. As an afterthought, he grabbed a small log from a nearby pile and placed it carefully beside the skull, marking it for a future visit.

They rounded the first bend in the road and Dawson glanced at John, now leaning his head against the passenger window. "You okay?"

John turned his head slowly and looked at Dawson silently. For a horrifying second, John's head morphed into the fractured skull and a hollow eye winked.

"What the fuck?" Dawson said, almost side-swiping a row of fir trees bordering the road. He gripped the wheel tightly with both hands and refocused on navigating the now dimly lit road as a crimson sun slowly dropped from the dark sky.

"Are *you* okay?" John asked. "What are you going off about?"

"Nothing." He didn't want to rattle his already rattled friend. They could discuss it back at the house, preferably over a couple of beers. Better still, a double shot of moonshine.

Dawson rounded the second bend in the road and began looking for landmarks. There should've been a huge white pine tree marking that corner. The pine needles from it should be on the road below, clear evidence of how the pine kills everything around it, except its own species, so that it might suck up all the water, thrive and prosper unobstructed. But there was no pine, no pine needles.

"What the fuck?" John said.

"I know," Dawson said. "This bend doesn't look like it should."

"I wasn't talking about that."

Dawson slowed and looked at his friend. "What were you talking about?"

"For a second there, you looked like that fractured skull we found near the fork. Scared the shit out of me."

Dawson slammed on the brakes.

"What're you doing?" John said.

"Are you kidding me?"

"No. You looked like that skull."

"Fuck, we better get out of here fast."

"Why?"

"So did you. When I looked at your earlier, you looked like that skull."

"Shit. This is starting to freak me out. And now you're saying that last bend didn't look familiar?"

"Not really. But it's getting dark. As you know, the road can be deceiving in the dark."

"Well, don't just sit there. Get your fucking truck moving."

Dawson didn't need much encouragement. He slammed the truck in Drive, and spun the tires as he took off. They drove in silence for the next minute, which, in the mired darkness of everything that had happened, seemed like a mini eternity to Dawson.

"There it is," Dawson said. "The pine I was looking for. Just misjudged it is all."

"Thank fucking God."

Passing the pine and its fallen needles, Dawson sighed deeply. Soon he came to another familiar bend, and another and another and another until finally they were out of the forest. He stopped in front of the barn to unload the chainsaws. He still had a lot to think about concerning what to do about the skull, and he needed a couple of stiff drinks to calm his nerves enough to come to a logical conclusion.

But, through the fear and confusion, an idea was already forming: get his tractor out first thing in the morning and line that ill-fated fork with four feet of good old red and reliable Prince Edward Island dirt. Bury the skull and forget about it. What could dragging it up now possibly accomplish?

"I better get going," John said. "My wife will be cooking dinner."

Dawson checked his watch. "I think you've missed dinner. It's a little past nine."

"What?" John said. He checked his watch. "Shit, you're right. But that's impossible."

Not again. More mysteries. Where's that fucking moonshine. "What do you mean?"

"I checked my watch before we left. It was exactly eight. Now it's five-past-nine. Are you saying it took a little over an hour for us to travel your one-mile beach road?"

"I didn't check the time," Dawson said. "I was so freaked out by that skull I didn't even think about it."

"Well, I did. And I know what I saw."

It occurred to Dawson that it *had* taken them longer than normal to reach the end of the road. But an hour and five minutes? *I don't think so.* But somewhere in the dark recesses of his troubled mind, he knew John was right. Even though John had just suffered a concussion.

"Are you sure?" Dawson said. "Remember, you took a pretty good wack to the head. Probably suffered a minor concussion. You yourself complained about dizzy spells afterward."

John's face tightened. "Dawson, for fuck sakes. I know what time it was when we left. And I think you got a pretty good fucking idea as well, you just refuse to believe it."

Dawson tugged on his thick beard. "I suppose you're right. Do me a favor, don't mention any of this to anybody. None of it, please. We still gotta figure out what to do with that skull."

"My lips are sealed," John said. "Besides, my wife would think I'm batshit crazy if I start telling her what happened."

"You want a ride home?" Dawson said. He knew he couldn't talk John into a drink, especially since he would probably already catch shit for being late for dinner. And even though he lived less than a thousand feet down the highway, Dawson still thought that given his friend's condition, it was a responsible and caring gesture on his part.

"Forget about it," John said, beeping open his pickup with a remote control. "I'll stop by tomorrow afternoon and we can talk."

"Have a great night. And thanks again for your help."

Halfway to his truck, John stopped and spun around. "Just put it on my bill."

***

Four shots of moonshine later, Dawson knew that his first idea about what to do about the skull was the right one. Use his tractor to shovel four feet of dirt over it, smooth it over, and then forget about it. He only hoped John would go along with his plan and would keep it a secret. No matter how many times he ruminated about the notion of reporting it to authorities, none of it made sense. Dawson didn't want government officials, cops, reporters, and nosey neighbors poking around his property wanting to take a peek at a man, or a woman, who'd probably died in a gunfight over a moonshine order gone wrong. There would be stories, there would be rumors, and his property would become known as a Prohibition-era cemetery, a tourist attraction. He didn't want throngs of uninvited people roaming around. Hell, maybe officials would even demand a large-scale excavation of the entire area, effectively killing any notion of peace, seclusion, and privacy.

He stared at the empty moonshine bottle as if it somehow held the answers to his dilemma. *It was all eerily related*, he thought. A moonshine distributor shot dead. Him drinking moonshine. He brushed the thought away, not liking at all where it might lead.

He was beginning to understand something. It was one thing to find a skull on your property, no, actually step on and fracture it. It was quite another to then figure out what to do with it. What if the skull didn't belong to a rum-running man from another era at all? What if it belonged to a more recent murder victim? *Impossible. I bought this property over fifteen years ago and nothing's changed back there unless I've changed it. Okay, then how about justice for a long dead moonshine runner?*

Maybe some closure for his family? Never mind. Live by the sword, die by the sword.

With that shaky resolve, Dawson decided it was long past his bed time. He went into the bathroom, splashed some cold water on his sweat-soaked face and beard, and towel-dried himself. As he hooked the towel onto its hanger, he glanced in the mirror. It was fleeting but frightening. His reflection transformed into a fractured, hollow-eyed skull and looked back at him with a maniacal grin.

"Fuck off," he said, goosebumps rushing up his spine and chasing him out of the bathroom.

A few minutes later, tossing fitfully in bed, he couldn't purge the terrifying thought from his mind. John had transformed into the skull. He had transformed into the skull. He was still turning into the skull. What did that mean?

Would it be a bad omen to let dead dogs lie?

***

"I did get some sleep but my dreams were terrifying," Dawson told John over beers the following evening. John had arrived one beer ago. They sat around a small campfire in Dawson's backyard. Dawson had yet to brief him on his new plan. He'd been too busy listening to John's frightful account of an insomnia-plagued night in which he couldn't get the image of the fractured skull out of his mind.

"But in spite of that, my little head injury is doing well," John said. "The bump is way down and, you're right, it was only a small cut. What did you dream about?"

"That I was a moonshine runner back in the day. I was armed with a pistol and I didn't hesitate to use it when confronted with a threat—either real or perceived."

"What, you walked around shooting people?"

"Something like that. It was eerily similar to the story Blaine told me about the gunfight that had erupted after the moonshine order somehow got fucked up. Except I wasn't the one delivering the order to the boats at the beach. I was on the boat near the beach. There to pick up the order. I guess I didn't trust the people delivering it so I opened fire. Killed about four of them."

"Man, that's pretty fucked up."

"Tell me about it."

"How did the nightmare end?"

"They started shooting back, and I turned the boat around. But not before going on shore and loading up the moonshine order. Without paying."

"Did you get away?"

"That's where it gets sketchy. I was getting away under heavy gunfire, and then I woke up. I only remember it because I wrote it all down right away."

"Is your family tree connected to any of the moonshine manufacturers who used to live here?"

"Not that I'm aware of." The truth was Dawson hadn't bothered to look into it. He had two brothers whom he didn't speak to much, and his relationship with his mother and father was civil but far from loving. There was no drama as far as he was concerned. He just wasn't religious and they were, so he preferred to distance himself.

"Have you decided what you want to do about the skull?"

"I think so. Did you tell your wife?"

"No."

"Good. Don't. Please."

John's eyebrows arched. "You mean you don't want to report this?"

Dawson explained his reasons for wanting to bury it under the rug. "And you'll get dragged into it too. You'll probably have stupid tourists poking around your property mistaking it for mine. Not to mention the news media, cops, and government officials bothering you."

John scratched the new bandage on his head as he sipped his beer. "Did you go down there today?"

"No. I wanted to wait to talk to you first." It was more than that, but Dawson wasn't ready to admit it right now. He was scared shitless.

"So, you really want to cover it in four feet of dirt and continue driving over it every time you go to the beach?"

"I don't need that fork to get to the beach. I'll block it off with a big dead tree and preserve it as a cemetery. Let it reforest itself naturally. Let dead dogs lie."

"You think you can live with that?"

"You got a better idea?"

"I don't know. Maybe it'll be a bad omen to bury it again. Maybe you'll be haunted by it every time you go to the beach."

"And maybe we'll be haunted by all the other fucks who'll show up if we report it. And I just thought of something. Don't you think it'll stigmatize my property if people learn I'm living in a cemetery for dead moonshine runners?"

"I suppose you're right. If it's stigmatized, it'll drop in value," John said.

"Exactly."

Watching the flickering flames spark hot embers up into the starry night sky, both men grew silent. It was as if the quietness meant a mutual understanding had been reached. A deal of sorts, shrouded in an unspoken but fully understood code of silence.

And John confirmed as much. "My lips are sealed, bro. I won't say shit about this to anyone. And I'll help you bury it if you want. I... I feel a part of this now. I've been haunted by the image of the skull probably as much as you have."

Dawson hadn't told John about his metamorphosis into the skull while glancing at his reflection in the mirror last night. But it didn't matter. They'd reached an agreement that would be executed first thing in the morning.

"Tomorrow morning at eight sharp?" Dawson said.

"Done."

"Let's have a toast," Dawson said, raising his beer. "To giving the dead man back his final resting place. So he might rest in peace."

"Cheers," John said.

They drained their beers at exactly the same time and tossed their cans toward a plastic garbage can leaning up against a large pine tree.

"Damn," John said. "We both missed."

"Don't worry," Dawson said. "We won't miss tomorrow."

An hour and two beers later, they retreated from the smoldering fire pit, deciding wisely not to overdo it the night before a funeral. Dawson waved at John as he drove away, sighing heavily as he entered his house. He felt a little tipsy and relieved that they had solved the fractured skull mystery.

It would be forever buried. Forever forgotten.

He closed and locked the door behind him.

As the deadbolt snapped into place with a comforting metallic click, a solitary dark cloud passed over the full moon, transforming it into the image of a grotesquely grinning skull. Then a deep-socketed and hollow eye winked and the menacing face vanished as quickly as it had emerged.

**

Dawson jammed his John Deere tractor into reverse, spinning around with a large load of dirt. He lurched forward, lowering the bucket expertly, and dumped a load over the entrance to the fork. He was about twenty feet away from the grave and wanted to create a gradual hill over the skull rather than risk disturbing the earth around it or crushing it. His night had been uneventful and he'd slept like a bear. But he couldn't exactly say the same thing about his morning. He'd woken with a bad case of the jitters, spilling his coffee, spraining his pinky finger while, of all things, picking up the pieces of his shattered coffee cup. And then, the icing on the cake, he'd noticed, if only for a fleeting moment, that his bearded lumberjack-looking face had once again morphed into the fractured skull. He'd hurried away from his bathroom mirror, unwilling to give the monster the satisfaction of winking at him yet again.

I'll be the one doing the winking, he thought, backing up and grinning as John gave him the thumbs up and pointed him toward another moss-covered dirt pile. He swooped in, lifted it, and deposited it.

Five minutes later, he was at the grave site dumping piles of dirt all around and over it. When he was satisfied with his work, he began smoothing it out, being careful to leave a hill of dirt over the site. He was starting to feel better already, knowing that he would be leaving the monster behind and leaving his nightmares in the dust.

After he finished, he backed the tractor up a few feet behind the new-and-improved grave site, killed the ignition, climbed off the tractor, and stood admiring his handiwork.

John approached from behind and tapped him on the shoulder. He spun around, residual nerves driving a sudden wave of panic through him.

John grinned, nothing like his usual look of amusement. "I scare you?"

"You did. Anyway, thanks for your help. I'm glad it's done."

A bottle of clear liquid suddenly appeared in John's right hand, two shot glasses in his left.

Dawson blinked several times, unable to believe his eyes. "Where... where did you get that?"

John raised the bottle, his maniacal grin widening. "This here moonshine? I made it."

"You make moonshine now?"

John ignored the question, instead passing Dawson a shot glass and popping the cork from the bottle with a flick of his thumb. The cork twirled high in the air and landed on the excavated dirt directly above the fractured skull, if Dawson's memory served. He suddenly wanted to leave the grave site, and damn fast.

But John began slowly pouring moonshine into Dawson's glass.

"It's only, like, eleven in the morning," Dawson said.

"Never mind," John said. He finished filling Dawn's glass and filled his own. "We should respect the dead, say a few words, and have a toast in celebration of our efforts, so that this poor soul may rest in peace."

"What do you want me to say?"

John moved closer and put his arm around Dawson's shoulder. A cold chill enveloped Dawson. John exhaled and Dawson grimaced as he was assaulted by John's breath—the scent of rancid death.

"Why don't you start by saying you're sorry?" John said.

"Sorry... sorry for what?"

John dropped the bottle on the ground and its contents cascaded over the mound covering the fractured skull. John's features morphed into a bloodied and battered skull. Dawson tried to struggle free from John's grip but an ice-cold hand powerfully squeezed the back of his neck.

"Sorry for stealing my moonshine," John said. "Sorry for shooting me in the fucking head."

A lightning bolt of fear shot through Dawson's body. *My dream. Shooting people and stealing moonshine. What the fuck?* "I don't know what the fuck you're talking ab... "

"Take your last drink," John demanded.

Not understanding why, Dawson drained the moonshine, making a face as its harsh bite stung his throat.

The ground beneath them suddenly began to crumble. The earth heaved up behind them, upending the tractor and sending it careening down on top of them. But before the heavy machine could crush them, the ground opened up and swallowed them.

Dawson felt himself falling, down, down, down, down, and heard a loud thud as his ass struck a hard surface below. As his vision adjusted to the light, he realized he was sitting at a candle-lit kitchen table, a bottle of moonshine in one hand, a full shot glass in the other.

He could suddenly make out his guest. Or was he the guest? The fractured skull grinned at him, raised a shot glass of moonshine, and said, "Let's drink to my revenge."

With a strenuous effort, Dawson steadied his breathing, trying to reassure himself that this was nothing more than a nightmare. He would wake up in his bed and have to bury the fractured skull all over again. The previous ritual was only a bad dream.

"I'll drink to that," Dawson said, draining the shot glass and slamming it down hard on the tabletop. It shattered in his hand. A million shards of glass danced slowly in the air, reflecting fragments of candlelight and shining a kaleidoscope of colors around the room. He examined his hand. *Not a scratch. Gotta be a nightmare.*

"This is no nightmare," John said. "And I'm not John. And you're not Dawson."

Dawson struggled to control his rising fear. "Who are you, then? And who am I?"

"I'm Seth Baxter and you're Red Cullen. During Prohibition, we delivered an order of moonshine to you and your cronies at the waterfront. You falsely claimed that we had shorted you. You put a bullet in my head and sailed off with the moonshine without paying. Stole it. For many years I lay restless in my grave, turning over in my grave, waiting for my revenge. When you fractured my skull, it awakened and unleashed the otherworldly powers of revenge, of karma, if you like. You finally got your just desserts."

A part of Dawson started to believe it. His terror slowly gave way to anger. Maybe that emotion was what it would take to get him out of this nightmare. His face tightened and he lunged at the skull, swinging a powerful right fist that went right through the grinning face as if it were merely a shadow of its former self. The errant punch sent Dawson careening into the wall. He covered his face with both arms and closed his eyes, trying to protect himself from what would probably be a painful face-plant. But his head and the front half of his body penetrated the wall seamlessly. He opened his eyes, looking around in horror at a tsunami-sized wall of flames rushing toward him. As he felt the heat getting more intense, he pulled himself back into the relative safety of the dungeon-like and old-fashioned kitchen.

Dumbfounded and horrified, he looked at the skull's hollow eye sockets. "This can't be happening. I'm not Red. I'm Dawson. I'm gonna wake up soon."

"No, you're not," Seth said, pouring another glass of moonshine. "Dawson doesn't exist. Dawson never existed. He was invented as a part of my plot for revenge."

Dawson, or Red, was becoming more frightened and consumed with each passing second. "What... what about Red?"

Seth drained his moonshine and slammed the glass hard on the table top. It shattered into smithereens, its fragments creating the same kaleidoscope of colors Red had seen earlier.

"Red—you, that is—died of natural causes almost twenty years after you killed me," Seth said. "You were never brought to justice for the cold-blooded murders you committed."

Seth refilled another glass with the potent hooch and raised it high in the air. "That is, until now. Now you can rot in hell where you've always belonged."

"No... no... no... please, no... please, God, wake me the fuck up."

The Black Hole

Virginia Stevens looked forward to her weekly get-togethers with Sophia Burlington. More than just the camaraderie and friendship, she enjoyed their intellectual discussions. Like Virginia, Sophia was a vibrant, curious, end energetic woman in her mid-thirties who loved trying to solve life's riddles and mysteries. Every Saturday they would meet at either Virginia's apartment or Sophia's flat, have dinner and a bottle of wine or two, and then spend the rest of the evening discussing and trying to solve life's conundrums. Sometimes the conversations became quite heated and other times they would be on the same page. But they always ended the evenings on a positive note, understanding full well that to preserve their 20-year friendship, they would have to agree to disagree. Last Saturday, they'd discussed ghosts and more specifically whether or not they believed in spectral entities. After some initial doubt, Sophia had come on board with Virginia's way of thinking—saying she believed in ghosts. When all else failed, Virginia pulled out her ace in the hole—the preponderance of evidence argument.

As Virginia stirred her pasta sauce, simultaneously watching the rotini pasta boil, she wondered how Sophia would weigh in on tonight's planned discussion—the black hole. Not the one that referred to the Bermuda Triangle, although that might come up in their discussion. No, they were gonna focus on the black hole as it relates to the psychological abyss. That point you reach in your life when you stare into the black hole, the abyss, and it stares back at you, a point of utter desperation, sadness, and helplessness.

Not that Virginia had anything to feel desperate, sad, or helpless about. She was a rising star in an ad agency and had been recently awarded a promotion for one of her creative genius ad campaigns. Sophia, as well, had nothing to be downtrodden about. She'd just inked a deal with one of the largest accounting firms in the city of Vancouver and had just made full partner. They were both attractive, upwardly mobile women.

Well, maybe there was just that one thing, Virginia thought, adjusting the heat on the pasta sauce to simmer, removing the boiling rotini, and draining it through a strainer in the kitchen sink. Neither of them had much interest in the opposite sex, both claiming that their last break-ups—Virginia's three years ago, and Sophia's four—had left indelible scars on their hearts which had contributed, if not spearheaded, distrust and a general dislike for the male species. They'd both agreed that for now that conversation was mostly off limits. Time would eventually heal their broken hearts and there was absolutely no reason whatsoever to rush it.

But in spite of her reassurances, Virginia frowned. She couldn't help feeling sad about it. Incomplete in some way. Maybe it was the lack of sex. Maybe it was a shortage of intimacy. She didn't know. However, on some level, she was certainly missing something. *Am I heading into the black hole? The abyss?*

Ding-dong! Ding-dong! Ding-Dong!

Virginia checked the time. 5:59 pm. Like clockwork, Sophia was one minute early. "Be right there."

She finished draining the steaming pasta, poured it into a large bowl, and answered the door. Her jaw just about dropped on the floor when she beheld her friend. Normally a conservative dresser at work and a casual dresser at play, Sophia looked absolutely stunning in a form-fitting black dress with a plunging neckline that accentuated pert breasts. Her three-inch black pumps added a touch of elegance and class to the look. Virginia noticed, not for the first time, that Sophia's curves were smooth, tight, and all in the right places. This, in contrast to her more buxom and full-figured body.

"My God," she said with a smile. "You look stunning."

Sophia grinned, brushed away an errant lock of her long and shimmering black hair, and hugged her friend warmly. The physical contact brought goosebumps to Virginia's body as she felt Sophia's breasts rub up against her own hardening nipples.

Virginia felt her cheeks flush hotly as she released her friend. "I'm embarrassed. Look at me, jeans and a frumpy t-shirt, and you dressed to kill."

Sophia removed a bottle of champagne from her hand bag. "That's okay, dear. I was just thinking that life's been so good to us lately, it calls for a little celebration. I thought maybe after dinner we can go for a drink. You can change later, but certainly not now." She winked. "I love you just the way you are."

After dinner and a few glasses of wine, they sat next to one another on a loveseat in Virginia's living room. For reasons not completely clear to her, Virginia found herself feeling self-conscious; unable to look directly at her friend without her eyes wandering around Sophia's shapely, toned, and half-exposed body. She deliberately kept looking out of her scenic seventh-floor apartment window at the glittering lights of downtown Vancouver.

Sophia sensed her unease. She leaned over, exposing a tantalizing amount of cleavage, and touched Virginia's shoulder. "Is something wrong, honey?"

Virginia felt a warm and tingly feeling between her legs. If she had lesbian tendencies in the past, she'd never known it. At least never inwardly contemplated it. Now she was being bombarded from another part of her psyche with questions about her own sexuality. And, she was having a hard time dealing with it. Then she got an idea.

"I know what it is," Virginia said. "I need to change."

She returned from her bedroom wearing a flowing and form-fitting red dress which also had a plunging neckline that revealed most of her large melon-shaped breasts. She'd also released her pony-tail and combed her long and curly hair blonde hair out. A few curly locks fell over her chest and the rest of the golden mane draped smoothly down her back. Virginia slowly smiled as she watched Sophia's adoring green eyes undress her from bottom to top, stopping and lingering for a long moment at the nakedness of her cleavage.

Sophia practically leaped from the loveseat, rushed over to Virginia, and hugged her tightly. The warmth and tingles that exploded through Virginia's breasts and between her legs was delightful. Sophia planted a wet kiss on Virginia's cheek as she released her. "You look gorgeous. I think I'll switch teams."

Virginia felt her cheeks heat up as she smiled. She was beginning to feel giddy with excitement. "Let's crack that champagne. What're we celebrating?"

Sophia removed the bottle from a bucket of ice on the coffee table and began twisting off the metal ring. "My partnership at the firm. Your promotion. No, how about our friendship?"

"How about all three?"

Pop!

The plastic cork bounced off the ceiling, ricocheted off a picture on the wall, and soared across the room, flying directly between the two of them, before bouncing off the opposite wall and rolling to a stop on the plush carpet.

They both erupted in laughter as champagne began bubbling out of the bottle.

"You first," Sophia said, holding the bottle to Virginia's open mouth. Virginia gulped mouthfuls of champagne as tiny foam rivers dribbled down her chest, staining her dress, and drenching her erect nipples.

Virginia grabbed the bottle, pushing it gently but quickly over to Sophia's waiting and wanting mouth. She pressed it between her lips.

Sophia took two long pulls as bubbly dribbled down her bare chest, a tiny river forking at her cleavage and streaming over her rock-hard nipples.

When they'd finished guzzling and laughing, they both sat down, legs touching, and Sophia filled two champagne flutes, offering one to Virginia with a seductive smile.

"To us, baby," Sophia said. "I'm so happy I have you in my life."

"Me too," Virginia said. She was giddy from the sudden release of sexual tension and the euphoria of the alcohol high.

As they nestled into the loveseat, and Sophia began to gently stroke Virginia's exposed leg, making her insane with excitement and anticipation, Virginia said, "What about the black hole? Are we gonna discuss that?"

Sophia moved in close, took Virginia's face gently in both hands, and planted a long, wet, tongue-probing, and passionate kiss on her lips. "The only black hole I can think about right now is the one I want to have my tongue deep inside of."

Sophia cupped one of Virginia's breasts, popped it loose, and began licking a large and swollen nipple.

A soft moan escaped Virginia's lips.

Virginia slid her hand along Sophia's slender thigh and moaned again when her fingers touched a dripping wet, sticky, and panty-free pussy.

"Oh... oh... oh," Sophia moaned, "yeah... just like that."

***

Driving over to Sophia's apartment a week after that steamy night, Virginia felt the butterflies dancing in the pit of her stomach, her palms and armpits perspiring with nervous anticipation. She hadn't spoken to Sophia for the entire week. The only communication between them had been a text message last night: *Are we still on for tomorrow.* To which, Virginia had answered in the affirmative and had then debated internally for the next half hour whether she should add, *I'm looking forward to it.*

In the end, she'd decided against that response, viewing it as too suggestive. She'd also debated her dinner party wardrobe selection for about an hour, struggling with whether to go hot-to-trot with a sexy dress, or err on the side of caution and dress more conservatively. In the final analysis, cautious optimism won the battle and she'd opted for tight blue jeans, a black V-neck long-sleeved blouse, and stylish black leather boots with two-inch heels. Since it was mid-autumn, she also wore a thin nylon white windbreaker, dotted with pink flowers.

In between her work schedule, she'd spent most of the week analyzing what had happened between the two of them and what it meant. Did this mean they were now an item? Were they both closet lesbians who'd smashed open the closet door and exploded passionately into embracing their new sexuality? Or, was this a one-off, never to be discussed again, never to be repeated again? And what did it mean for their long-time intimate friendship if that were the case? Would it damage their relationship? Would it create a cold and reserved tension in their otherwise easy and intimate friendship?

Virginia didn't have any of the answers and, although the passionate evening with Sophia had rocked her to the core, she didn't know if ultimately women were her thing on a full-time, permanent, and monogamous basis. The odd fling, sure why not? But a full-time same-sex relationship? She didn't know if she was ready for that right now.

She pulled into the parking lot of Sophia's apartment complex, found a parking stall, and turned off the ignition. She checked her hair in the rear-view mirror, and pushed a curly lock aside, deciding she was happy at least with her hairstyle choice—long, flowing, and combed out to look like a golden horse mane.

She pressed 769 at the building's entrance and the speaker squawked before Sophia's melodic voice asked, "Is that you, Virginia?"

"Yeah."

Bzzzzzzzzzzzzzzzz.

She knocked three times on the door and nervously wiped her perspiring palms on her jeans while waiting for Sophia to answer.

A small soft voice from the other side. "It's open. Come on in."

The block of ice engulfing Virginia melted into warm water after Sophia, also dressed cautiously optimistic, embraced her with a tight warm hug and kissed her gently on the cheek.

Over a bottle of white wine, they got caught up on the week's events, mostly discussing office politics and work accomplishments.

Finally, Virginia, unable to contain the suspense, said, "Do you think we need to discuss what happened?"

Sophia's lips tightened before creasing into a small frown. "I suppose we do. I was, I don't know, kind of embarrassed about it all week, so I couldn't bring myself to talk to you."

"Me too."

And, anyway, I didn't want to discuss it over the phone."

"Me neither."

"So what do we do?" Sophia said. Her tone was tight, tense.

"I don't know," Virginia said, lobbing the ball back in her court. "What do you want to do?"

"I never thought I was a lesbian, so maybe it's just a one-off. What do you think?"

"Those are my thoughts as well."

"You mean you'd rather be with a man?"

"Possibly. I'm confused about that."

"Me too," Sophia said. "But, I have to tell you, it was so fucking incredible."

Goosebumps sprang up on Virginia's arms and she rubbed them smooth. "I know. That's the problem. But I don't know if I wanna get involved in anything that might ruin our friendship. It's too valuable to me."

"That's how I feel," Sophia said, stroking Virginia's arm, seemingly in an effort to help her flatten the goosebumps.

Virginia nervously removed her own hand from her own arm and Sophia, taking the cue, also removed hers.

"It sounds like we both need more time to process our feelings before going any further," Virginia said.

Sophia nodded with a smile. "Why don't we do that? Take a month and see how we feel. If, at the end of the month, one feels one way and one feels the other, we'll agree to disagree and won't let it ruin our friendship. Or, who knows, we may decide that we like the odd fling with each other and still decide to pursue men on the side."

After a long pause, Virginia smiled and raised her wine glass. She knew it could be complicated if they eventually decided on a relationship that allowed them to share sexually intimate adventures with each other while also pursuing men. Jealousy could rear its ugly head. Anything could happen. But, given their similar feelings and emotions on the subject, it still appeared like the right decision. Besides, if Sophia eventually were to decide that an open relationship was what she wanted with Virginia, Virginia could always gently veto the idea if that was where her heart eventually led her.

"I'll go along with that," Virginia said. "Let's drink to it."

"Cheers," Sophia said, raising her glass. They clinked glasses gently, simultaneously set them on the table, and hugged.

After a delicious Chinese dinner of beef and broccoli fried rice, curry beef brisket, and sweet and sour pork, they returned to the living room to discuss the black hole. Out of respect for their new agreement, Virginia sat in an armchair opposite her friend.

Sophia started the discussion. "What do you think of when you hear the black hole?"

Virginia crossed her legs self-consciously, flashbacks of last Saturday's lasciviousness dancing teasingly in her mind. *The only black hole I can think about right now is the one I want to have my tongue deep inside of.* "Well, obviously the Black Hole can refer to the Bermuda Triangle." *Triangle? Even that sounds suggestive.* "But people use it in other contexts as well. Psychologists, for example, sometimes use the black hole and the abyss synonymously. It's a place where some people don't wanna go. That point you reach in your life when you stare into the black hole, the abyss, and it stares back at you, a point of utter desperation, sadness, and helplessness. I'm sure you've heard the saying, 'I stared into the abyss and the abyss stared back.'"

"Yeah, I get that," Sophia said. "It's almost like a metaphor for our dark demons that we're unwilling to come to grips with."

"The skeletons in our closets," Virginia said.

"Exactly. So, getting back to my question, is that what it means to you? Skeletons in your closet that you're unable to confront?"

Virginia was starting to relax again and enjoy the conversation. Sophia had the uncanny ability to help her discover her own unresolved truths and she fully understood recognition, rather than denial, was the first step to healing. "Yeah, I think it does. Tell me, what does the black hole mean to you?"

Sophia uncrossed her legs. A grin flashed across her face. "Well, certainly not the Bermuda Triangle. How about your love triangle?"

Virginia was raising her wine glass to her lips and she spilled a few drops on her exposed chest. She burst into laughter and so did Sophia.

When the laughter had subsided, Sophia said, "I was only joking."

"I know." But Virginia also knew that jokes almost always contained an element of truth. Nevertheless, she tried to push forward. "Seriously, what does the black hole mean to you?" *Am I begging for a repeat of the same answer?*

"Actually, I look at it more as something unknown and unknowable. But that doesn't make your interpretation any less valid or valuable."

There was a can of worms to be opened, but Virginia didn't know if she wanted to go there. Previously, the conversation had been off limits. *Why not?* she thought. Part of the reason for their intellectual problem-solving talks was to solve the world's problems as well as their own. "So based on my interpretation—skeletons in your closet that you refuse to confront—where do you stand?"

"What do you mean?"

"What skeletons have you not confronted?"

Sophia leaned back into the plush couch and thought for a moment. "I have issues with men. You know that. And so do you. We've made a choice not to discuss it. Remember?"

Virginia nodded. "Do you think it's time to change that?"

Sophia scratched her dainty chin. "Probably, if you think about it. My split happened about four years ago and yours I believe was three."

"That's right," Virginia said, steeling herself to release her demons into the atmosphere. "Do you wanna go first?"

"Okay." A long pause. "It's been so long since I've talked about this."

"If you're not ready we can do it another time."

"No. I wanna get this off my chest. I was with Brent for five years. We had our lives all planned out. A few kids, a nice home in the suburbs, both pursuing our careers and juggling family and relationship. What I didn't realize is that the whole time he was fooling around on me. Then he comes to me one day like a lost puppy dog and starts telling me he likes non-monogamous consensual relationships. That that's who he really is. I guess that's becoming popular now. Then he says he has three other girlfriends, all of whom know about me but I don't know about them. Then he has the gall to say that he wants me to agree to this type of relationship with him and even wants me to participate in a threesome with two of his girlfriends."

"My God," Virginia said. "What a scumbag. You think he could've told you that up front."

"Tell me about it."

"What did you do?"

"Told him to get the fuck out of my life forever."

"Is that what happened?"

Sophia nodded. "For about two months. Then I got drunk one night and called him over. He showed up with one of his girlfriends and I participated in a threesome. Last Saturday, when I slept with you, it was the second time I've slept with a woman."

"For me it was the first."

"Really? Anyway, the next day I woke up feeling guilty and embarrassed as hell and cut everything off, this time for good. But you know what the ironic thing is?"

Virginia thought she did but pleaded ignorance. "No."

"I enjoyed the sex with Pamela, his other girlfriend, way more than I ever enjoyed sex with Brent. Anyway, I've been struggling with my sexuality for years afterward, until you came along."

This really was turning into touchy territory. What did Sophia mean by that? That she was beginning to realize she wanted a female partner as opposed to a male? Virginia sidestepped the issue. "I guess it's my turn."

Sophia sipped wine, a small frown creasing her lips. "Go for it."

"Mine was just straight infidelity. I caught Barker sleeping with another woman in my old apartment of all places."

"What happened?"

"To give you some background, we'd been together for almost three years. I was the one pressing to take the relationship to the next level and he was always standoffish about that. It took me a while, but I finally realized why. He was fucking anything that moved."

"What, men and women?"

"I believe just women."

"Go on."

Virginia took a sip of liquid courage. She felt all the old wounds beginning to resurface, stabbing her in the heart like a hundred tiny needles. She cleared her throat and continued. "One night Parker slept at my apartment. He had a day off and I had to work overtime. I thought I'd surprise him at lunch time and I brought home some take-out Mexican food. I opened the apartment door to find him screwing another woman up the ass on my living room couch."

"What an asshole," Sophia said. "I'm sure you kicked them both out there and then."

Virginia nodded. "I did a little more than that. I threw their clothes out on the street and threw them out practically buck-naked."

"Ever hear from him since?"

"No. And I've never contacted him, not even in a weak drunken moment."

"I don't blame you," Sophia said. "Sometimes I wish we could take revenge on these fuckers and tear them a new asshole."

"In some ways I think we've taken our revenge," Virginia said.

"How?"

"I hardly give men the time of day right now. I snub them. And I bet you do the same. An attractive woman like yourself, how many times have you been asked out since Brent?"

"Exactly twelve," Sophia said.

"See, you even keep track," Virginia said. "And all twelve have been met with rejection, am I right?"

Sophia nodded. "And sometimes not too kindly. How many times have you been asked out since fuck face?"

"Thirteen."

"You keep track as well."

"I do. And all of my suitors have been rejected—some in rather harsh terms."

"So, we're getting our revenge," Sophia said, frowning.

"Yeah, we're taking our hatred of our exes out on the male population."

After a long pause, Sophia said, "You know what that makes us, right?"

"Unfortunately, I do," Virginia said. "It makes us pretty fucked up."

Sophia put her glass on an end table and cradled her face in her hands. Virginia saw a tear drop from her lower eyelid and streak down her face. She was about to rush to her friend's aid but was aware of where it might lead and didn't think, in light of the painful confessions and sad conclusion, it was the right thing to do.

Finally, Sophia looked at Virginia. She was a mask of sadness and despair. "What should we do?"

"I don't know. We can get counseling. We can accept the next dates we're asked out on." *Maybe we should get our sexual kicks and intimacy with each other and tell men to go fuck themselves.* "Maybe we should go to a bar, pick up some men, and fuck our brains out just to get it out of our system."

A mischievous grin slowly erased Sophia's sad expression. "You think that would work?"

"It won't hurt. We obviously both have men issues."

***

"He's kind of cute," Virginia said, pointing discreetly.

They sat on barstools at the bar at Brannigan's, a popular Vancouver pick-up joint. They'd planned on going out for a drink previously but had decided to postpone it to give them more time to mentally prepare. Instead of the usual home-cooking, they'd dined out about an hour earlier and already had shared a bottle of white wine over dinner. Virginia had been happy for the delay, even happier that last week their evening had ended on a positive and friendly note, with none of the sexual intimacy they'd shared previously at Virginia's apartment. The night had ended with a hug, a peck on the cheek, and that was that. It seemed they were both just a little too confused to let it escalate beyond that.

Sophia studied the man Virginia had pointed to. A tall lean man dressed in black leaned against a table at the window. He had mid-length dark and wavy hair and high cheekbones. He talked animatedly with his friend, waving his hands to make his point.

"You mean that man in black, right?" Sophia asked.

"Yeah."

"I like his friend. Kind of a bookish, intellectual-looking."

"You ladies like another one?" the bartender said, noticing their virtually empty wine glasses. He was a bear of a man with bushy black hair and a full beard.

"Sure," Virginia said, and he began pouring wine.

He set the drinks down in front of them, grinned bearish, and went to attend to another customer in the crowded locale.

"Well, should we approach them?" Virginia asked.

"We don't want to appear desperate," Sophia said. "Let's give them the eye for a bit and see what happens."

Virginia nodded and flirted with her eyes for a few seconds before turning to Sophia. "Nothing yet. Your turn."

As Sophia ran a hand through her hair, she struck a pose, smiling toward the two men at the window.

For the first time, Virginia noticed, she and Sophia's outfits were almost identical: jeans, knee-length black leather boots, red V-neck blouses, and smart black blazers. She'd probably been too nervous earlier to have given it much thought.

"Any luck?" Virginia asked.

Sophia grinned and raised her wine glass to her lips. "I think I'm getting some attention from Bookish. But he's shy. He looked away right away."

"We could almost pass for sisters," Virginia said.

"I noticed that earlier but didn't want to say anything. Some women hate it when others dress the same as them."

"I'm not one of them."

"For me to be your sister, I'd have to go from black to blonde, fill out a bit more, and grow my boobs out."

They both laughed. Out of the corner of her eye, Virginia caught the bartender gawking at her. Before attending to another customer, he shot her an almost imperceptible wink and a nod.

Sophia noticed it as well. "I think he likes you."

Virginia smiled and looked toward the window. The men had left. She glanced around and saw that they had circled and were now bee-lining it right toward them. As chance would have it, the two barstools next to Sophia and Virginia were empty.

"Don't look now," Virginia said, touching Sophia's hand softly. "We've got company."

The tall blackly attired man stepped right between Virginia and Sophia and pointed to the empty stools. "Excuse me, ladies, but do you mind if we sit here?"

"Go ahead," Virginia said with a twinkle in her eye.

"Thank you," the man said. He quickly introduced himself as Simon Brown and introduced his friend as Cray Wiseman. The women gave their names and handshakes and greetings were exchanged. Simon asked the women what they were drinking and then, not taking no for an answer, ordered a round of drinks.

The bartender delivered them with a frown and Simon slid them over the ladies.

Cray sat down, almost out of the conversational ring, and Simon remained standing, eyeballing Virginia with lascivious intentions. "I haven't seen you girls in here before. You from around these parts?"

Virginia had heard stupider opening lines, but that one was certainly in the top ten. *Don't be so harsh. Don't let your issues get in the way.* "I guess we don't get out much. We're both native Vancouverites."

"Yeah, we're a bit reclusive," Sophia said, her eyes drifting to Cray, who'd begun to peel the label off his Budweiser beer.

They got through some of the usual small talk, with Sophia becoming less and less interested as she began to study Cray. As Simon was explaining to them what he did for a living, Sophia finally made her move, moving over to Cray and taking the empty stool next to him.

"What do you mean, you 'sell shit?'" Virginia asked. A small ripple of unease and anxiety had begun to wash over her, and in an instant, she'd decided to expose this clown for who he was. *Always trust your gut.* "That could mean anything. What, you buy hot goods and fence them?"

"No, no, nothing like that. I own a pawn shop on Main Street. I buy desperate people's goods and sell them for a profit."

"In other words, you exploit people." Virginia had also read news reports of Vancouver pawn shops doing just that; buying hot goods and fencing them. And until a recent police crackdown, many of them had been getting away with it.

A few wrinkles spread across Simon's brow and his thin lips tightened. Then he grinned broadly. "I don't look at it like that. I help people who are desperate and buy their crap. I have to sell it for a profit. We're a business after all."

His response seemed reasonable, Virginia thought. Maybe she was just being hyper-sensitive. "I suppose that's true. What's the name of your pawn shop anyway?"

Simon chewed on the corner of his lower lip for a second before responding. "Hey, I don't wanna bore you with business. That's not what you came here for is it?"

"What's that supposed to mean?"

"I'm not blind. I saw you looking at me earlier. Smiling at me. Flirting with me."

Virginia squirmed in her seat. Simon remained standing and had yet to occupy the empty stool next to her. Meanwhile, she noticed Sophia and Cray exchanging many laughs and demonstrating highly suggestive body language.

Weren't they on a mission? Did she want to be a stick in the mud?

Without waiting for a reply, Simon leaned in and brushed her shoulder ever so lightly. Virginia couldn't decide if the goosebumps racing down her arm were a good or bad sign. Then he whispered in her ear, "You girls are giving off a Come-fuck-me vibe."

"That's a little presumpt—"

Before she could finish, Sophia was tugging at her arm. "Let's go. We're moving this party to my place."

***

After two glasses of wine at Sophia's second-floor apartment, she'd retired to the bedroom with Cray, who'd proven to be more amusing than Virginia had first given the diminutive little man credit for. His dry wit had them laughing through most of the last hour. Even Simon had mellowed from his earlier aggression and had switched into charm mode. He'd commented on how nice the apartment was, how pretty the women were, and how great the wine was.

Virginia began to hear soft moans emanating from Sophia's bedroom.

Simon took his cue and sat beside Virginia on the couch.

"You don't mind, do you?"

She was starting to become giddy, even a little horny, from the wine. "No."

He put his arm around her. "Good."

Something about his skin—cold and clammy—made her wriggle.

"Don't worry," he said. "I won't bite you. Not unless you want me to."

The alarm bell that had sounded loudly in Virginia's head earlier had now been muted to a dull roar; partly due to the alcohol; partly due to a determination to end her hatred of men once and for all. One part of her was worried about who he really was. The other part just wanted to get it over with. After all, Sophia was already screwing her brains out and it *had* been Virginia's idea to go out, pick up some men, and fuck their brains out—the first step to resolving their men issues. Yet she didn't feel all that turned on by Simon, not to mention all her other reservations.

That changed when he slipped his hand down her top, slid it inside her bra, and gently pinched her right nipple. She felt it harden in spite of her misgivings. His dark eyes locked with hers. "Your friend said there's an extra bedroom. Shall we?"

Virginia took him by the hand and guided him into the spare bedroom. Alcohol-fueled resolve had won the battle. She went over to the nightstand, flicked on a lamp, and dimmed the light to seductive. She heard Simon close the door behind them as she began peeling off her clothes.

By the time she had removed her top and bra, Simon was already on top of her, smothering her pendulous breasts with kisses. He moved his tongue over an erect nipple, clamped his teeth on it, and bit down hard.

"Ooww, that hurts. What're you doing?"

With one hand, he grabbed her by the throat and squeezed tightly. "Don't give me that, bitch. All women like it rough and you're no exception. So fucking high and mighty..."

***

Sophia couldn't believe that Cray was fucking her with his fly down and pants still on. But she'd been enjoying it so much she hadn't actually given it much thought. It had been over four years since she'd felt a man's penis inside of her and the smooth-gliding in-and-out sensation she was feeling now was as good, perhaps even better considering the time delay, as she'd remembered it.

Moaning, she moved her hand down to the small of his back, just above the waistline, and felt something hard and cold.

She gasped, realizing it sure as hell wasn't his dick. She tried to wrestle it free.

But he'd obviously felt her feel it. In a smooth motion, he slid off the bed, freed the gun, and leveled it at her head. "You weren't supposed to see that until later."

"What... what're you doing?"

The bookish nerd persona vanished and anger flashed across his face. "We're here to rape and rob you. But we didn't have to do the rape part. You two sluts went along with the sex willingly."

Sophia clenched her teeth and saw red. She acted on instinct, throwing a pillow at Cray, leaping from the bed, and kicking the gun out of his hands.

His eyes widened, startled at the lightning speed of her reaction. He dropped to the floor, scrambling to get the gun. She brought a well-timed kick directly to his jaw and heard a satisfying bone-snapping crack as he whimpered like the dog that he was and rolled over onto his back from the force of the blow.

Sophia bent down and reached for the gun.

The haze surrounding Cray's head cleared enough for him to crawl toward the weapon.

"No you don't," Sophia said, stomping on his outstretched hand.

She heard another series of satisfying snaps. Bones breaking. Fingers breaking.

"Oww, you fucking bitch," Cray said. "I'll kill you."

***

From repeated blows, Virginia's left eye was swollen shut. She could barely see out of the other eye. Her nose was bleeding badly. Her lower lip was cut and bleeding. After punching her into a state of near unconsciousness, Simon got up and began to peel off his pants.

Virginia, her arms hanging limply at her sides, could scarcely see him through the fog. But she still had her voice.

"Fuck you," she said.

"No, it's the other way around. I'm gonna fuck you like you've never been fucked before. Rough and violent. Just like you like it, bitch. Just like all women like it."

He approached the bed and climbed in next to Virginia. He put one hand on her throat and squeezed. With the other hand, he clamped both of her wrists together tightly. Then he mounted her, preparing to enter.

Kapow! Kapow! Kapow!

At the sound of gunshots, Simon released Virginia's hands and neck, arched his back, and turned toward the door. Virginia raked her long fingernails down his face and grinned as the ensuing fountain of blood splattered her face and bare breasts.

Sophia burst into the room, leveled the gun at his head with both hands, and shot Simon twice in the head.

***

One year and two weeks later.

It had been a traumatic and stressful ordeal, but both women had never been charged with murder. An act of self-defense. Simple as that. What made it easier was both men had rap sheets a mile long. They'd both done time for rape and robbery and were also wanted for questioning in connection with the rape, robbery, and murder of two women.

Virginia sat on her couch pondering how much her life had changed since the incident. From once being stressed out about her men issues, she now steadfastly just didn't trust men or even like them. She had no interest in them sexually. Even her therapist had tacitly agreed with her conclusions, although she couched it in different terms: "You are coming to grips with your sexuality."

Sophia's melodious voice from the kitchen: "Dinner's almost ready. How's your wine, hon?"

Virginia's glass was half full, as was her new-and-improved attitude about life, particularly about where her life was going. "I'm good, sweetheart."

Indeed, Virginia had a new sweetheart. A mere two weeks after the deaths of the two losers, they'd consummated their relationship; passionately, committedly, and monogamously falling into each other's arms. To make it legit, they'd mutually decided to sell Sophia's condo—too many bad memories. After it sold, Sophia moved in with Virginia. That was the plan for now. Eventually they planned on escaping the rat race to a nice home in the country.

Eating dinner a few minutes later, Sophia set her chopsticks down and produced a small white box decorated with a pink ribbon and bow, and placed it on the table.

"What's that?" Virginia said, arching an eyebrow.

"It's an anniversary gift. You do realize it's our one-year anniversary?"

Virginia hadn't forgotten. Neatly wrapped in a box hidden under the bed, there was a gold ring and a pair of stylish silver earrings—earmarked for her partner. She'd planned on breaking the news a little later when things became more intimate. "Yes. I have a surprise for you as well. It's in the bedroom."

"I love surprises," Sophia said with a grin. "Especially ones that involve me and you in the bedroom."

Virginia reached for the box. "Should I open it?"

"Of course."

Virginia peeled off the pink ribbon and bow and opened the box. Her mouth dropped open when she saw it. "A... a gun."

"It's not just any gun, my dear. It's a Glock 19. Commonly used by law enforcement. Made by an Austrian manufacturer that prides itself on quality."

After she got over the initial shock, she smiled. Surely after what they'd been through together, Sophia had bought it for protection and nothing more. "Thanks so much, honey. No one's gonna mess with us now."

"You're welcome," Sophia said, raising her glass. "Let's drink to our one-year anniversary. To many more years of love and happiness together."

"Cheers," they said in unison.

Virginia reached over and clinked glasses. After they drank, Sophia got up and wrapped Virginia in a tight embrace, planting a long and wet kiss on her lips.

After she returned to her seat, Sophia raised her glass again, a mischievous grin illuminating her face. "I have another toast."

Virginia giggled. "So many surprises. What're we drinking to now?"

Sophia's face tightened, her eyes going hard and cold. "Fuck men!"

Virginia slowly raised her glass and then lowered it suddenly. *Has she gone mad?* "You mean that figuratively of course."

Sophia's hardened expression held. "No. I mean we literally fuck men and then fuck them up... just like those losers did to us."

Screw Xmas

"Screw Xmas," Hank Weimer told his sister Andrea. "And, no, I won't accept your Xmas dinner invitation."

"You shouldn't talk like that," she said.

"Why not? That's how I feel. It's a stupid holiday."

"Why do you say that?"

"People you never ever hear from and never talk to send you stupid Xmas cards. What a bunch of bullshit. Phony bullshit."

"Well, aside from its religious significance, it's also a special time to get together with family and friends. You know, share special moments and all that."

"And all that," Hank said. "And all that bullshit. It's a terrible time of year. The malls go crazy, retailers go crazy. Commercialism runs rampant. People buy shit for people they normally wouldn't even talk to. A pair of socks, a pair of underwear, a box of chocolates. They max out credit cards and spend money they don't even have."

"You don't have to focus on the materialistic part of it," Andrea insisted. "That's why we draw straws."

Maybe she had a point, Hank thought, but he wasn't willing to acknowledge it. This year, from his family of three brothers and two sisters, he'd drawn Andrea's straw; technically, that meant only one gift. But could he really ignore his sister Karen's three toddlers? By the same token, could he ignore his brother Brandon's twin ten-year-old boys? Could he reasonably expect to ignore his mother and father, knowing most of his other siblings wouldn't? No, the whole thing was just fucked.

"I just don't like Xmas," he said. "Actually, I hate it."

"Well, you should try and change up your attitude a bit. And I know your reasons are much more deep-seated than what you let on. You should learn to get over it. And, I know why you always pronounce it Xmas even though it's Christmas. You want to make a mockery of the holiday. Stop that, will you?"

"Merry fucking Xmas," Hank said, pressing END CALL and slamming the phone down.

Feeling angry and irritated, he went into the kitchen of his modest one-bedroom apartment in downtown Vancouver, snatched a Coke from the refrigerator, and returned to the living room. He went over to the window and looked outside on that dreary Saturday afternoon. It was December 14th, and there was a steady and insidious drizzle coming down. It had been raining all day today and all day and night yesterday. *Welcome to the west coast of Canada in* the *winter.* On the busy street below, a few umbrella-holding pedestrians moved along, going about their daily tasks, whatever the hell they might be. Cars swished through puddles, grinding slowly down the busy street. Even on a Saturday, it was wall-to-wall traffic.

He sat down on his favorite tattered armchair, popped the tab on his Coke can, and briefly thought about doing some channel-surfing. He moved his hand toward the TV remote but abruptly changed his mind. He'd torn a lower back muscle at his shipper-receiver warehouse job two weeks ago and had been practically doing nothing but staring mindlessly at the Idiot Box for the last ten days. Laid up indoors on sick leave, he was fast becoming bored out of his mind. Worse still, due to the severity of the injury, he was under doctor's orders to rest for at least another two weeks before even attempting any exercise.

He ran a hand through his thick black hair and adjusted his glasses, which lately had started to slide down the bridge of his nose. Time for an adjustment, he knew. But not now. Now he could only do short walking stints around his apartment before the pain would stab his lower back, protesting loudly for him to sit his thirty-seven-year-old skinny ass back down. He grabbed a nearby pill bottle, popped the tab, and stuck two Ibuprofen pills in his mouth, washing them down with a mouthful of Coke and burping loudly.

It began to occur to him that he might have upset his sister. Andrea had just gotten married to a successful lawyer. They'd just purchased a brand-new home in the suburbs and were now planning a family. She had just married the love of her life, had just started a new career as a radiographer. She had everything to look forward to, especially around Xmas, a holiday he knew she loved. As a child he remembered how she could barely contain her excitement on Xmas Eve, eagerly anticipating waking up to all those presents under the tree. She would wake shouting with glee, and all ear-to-ear smiles. Her enthusiasm and happiness were infectious and would instantly spread through the entire family.

But not today, Hank thought glumly. *At least not for the moment. I just pissed in her cornflakes.*

He reached for his cell phone, suddenly feeling guilty and remorseful, like he owed Andrea an apology. After all, she'd done nothing wrong. All she'd wanted to do was cheer her brother up for the holidays. What was so wrong with that?

He started to punch in her number and stopped. *Fuck it. She'll get over it. She always does.* He set the phone down and tried to think of other things to think about, other things to do. Maybe he could call a friend to come over and watch a movie? *Who ya gonna call? Ghostbusters.*

Hank's friend list wasn't exactly extensive if you didn't count family. There was Mitch Silver, who, at 46, worked as a carry-out boy at a local grocery store. He'd just left for Ontario to spend Xmas with his family and all he really liked to do in his spare time was play video games and watch chick flicks. Strange combination, but it worked for Mitch.

There was Ryan Boddington, who'd lately taken a fancy to drinking excessively and trying to get laid on internet sex-hookup sites. *How's that working for ya, Ryan? Pick any hotties up while you're shit-faced?* He doubted it. In his last conversation with Ryan, Hank learned that five of the eight sites Ryan had once subscribed to had banned him for lewd and offensive behavior. Not a good role model to say the least.

Then there was Deborah Brasher, a likable and good-looking thirty-something woman, who had expressed some interest in Hank after he'd met her in a downtown coffee shop almost a year ago to the day.

However, even her interest had begun to wane after Hank mentioned to her a week ago over coffee that, "Xmas is for kids. Period."

And that was Hank being polite.

After reminding Hank that Christmas represented the birth of Jesus Christ, Deborah called it "a special time to express your love and devotion to friends and family."

Then she continued to gush over the holiday. Maybe it was his dead-pan expression while listening to her parade of positivity. Hank wasn't sure. Whatever it was, she'd stopped abruptly in mid-sentence, frowned, and said, "I don't think you really care about any of this. I think it's time for me to go."

So clearly, contacting Deborah Brasher, especially in the mood he was in now, wasn't a good idea. He extended his fingers, ready to count down all the digits of his other good friends. But no one, besides family, came to mind. The sad fact was that Hank no longer had a lot of friends. Many of them had moved away, and others he'd just lost contact with, as people often do.

And family wouldn't work right now. They were all crazy-happy over Xmas and Hank wasn't in the mood for any Xmas cheer right now.

So he dimmed the lights and wallowed in self-pity. Pity over the overwhelming depression that settled over him every Xmas. Pity that he was suffering way too much chronic pain to even go for a long walk and stop for a coffee or a drink. Even if he was well enough, *who wants to go out in this soup?*

Absently, Hank picked up his cell phone and scrolled through the contacts. Nothing, no one, zero, zilch, zip, nada.

Even though it was only 8:30 in the evening, he decided it was time to call it a night. He slowly rose, wincing as a sharp pain stabbed him in the back. *Pretty bad when you're so bored and depressed and in so much pain that all you want to do is sleep. What a life. Fuck life. Fuck Xmas.*

***

Hank was nine years old all over again, playing in the backyard of his suburban home with his sister, Lisa, born a year behind him. She was the one who looked so much like him and acted so much like him. Many people had commented that they could've been twins. Lisa was really a more refined and feminine version of himself, he realized as he watched her swing back and forth in the swing set.

He looked around the snow-covered backyard on that bright and sunny mid-December day. Where were his other siblings? Why weren't they out playing? But did it really matter? He always had the most fun with Lisa.

He stuck a twig in the nose area of the snowman he was making and turned to Lisa. "What do you think?"

Lisa laughed. "Use something else," she said. "It's too big and skinny. It's like a Pinocchio nose."

Hank giggled. "You're right. I'll wait for you to help me."

"Push me," Lisa said with a wry grin. "I want to go high. Way, way high."

Hank approached Lisa and positioned himself behind her on the swing. He started slowly, and soon had her soaring high in the air.

Back and forth. Back and forth. Higher and higher.

She giggled with delight. "Now I know what I wanna be when I grow up."

"What do you wanna be?"

"I wanna fly a plane and be a pilot. I love going higher and higher. Weeeeeeeeeee... I love it... weeeeeee..."

"A pilot? That's dangerous, isn't it?"

"Weeeeeeee... it doesn't matter. It'll be fun. Don't you think?"

"Sure, it'll be fun, just like this."

"Make me go higher, Hank. I wanna go higher."

"I'm getting scared. I don't want you to go too high."

"Come on, don't be a chicken. Just a little higher."

"Okay."

Hank backed up a little, allowing himself more pushing and pulling power, and soon had Lisa swinging a good three feet higher.

"How's that?" he said.

"I love it... I love it... weeeeeeeee..."

The back door of the house opened and Hank's mother poked her head out. "Come in now, kids. It's lunch time."

Hank removed his eyes from Lisa and looked at his mother for a fraction of a second, but that's all it took. On its backward momentum, the metal seat of the swing smacked him in the head and knocked him down. As a constellation of concussive stars danced around his head, blurring his vision and dulling his senses, he saw Lisa flying through the air. As the lights of consciousness dimmed, he felt warm blood trickle into his left eye and saw his sister plummeting to the ground head-first.

"No... Lisa!!"

He heard a loud blood-curdling scream and then everything went black.

***

He opened his eyes slowly and brought his hand to his head. *What?* It was wrapped in gauze. His eyes slowly adjusted to the powerful white light and he tried to focus. For a moment he saw only a shadowy image, undulating and indistinct.

Then the image changed. Blue eyes. Soft, pale skin. Shoulder-length golden blond hair. A small and dainty nose. And lips pursed in an expression of concern.

Then a voice. "Hank, you had a little accident. You're gonna be okay."

Confused, disoriented, and precipitously terrified, he bolted upright in bed. "What happened? Who are you?"

As soon as she smiled and those two dimples danced across her pretty face, he recognized her instantly. But she had aged. Albeit gracefully, but aged nonetheless. She must be at least as old as he was. *No, right. A year younger.* How could that be? She was dead, had died in that terrible swing accident that Hank could never stop blaming himself for.

"Lisa," he said. "Is it really you?"

She bent over, hugged him warmly, and pecked him on the cheek. Then she sat down on a chair that magically appeared bedside. "It's me, dear brother, and I want you to know something."

It took a moment for Hank to overcome the incredulity of the situation and get over his shock. It took another moment for him to compose himself enough to speak. He was being bombarded by strong and powerful feelings of love and well-being.

Finally, Hank said, "What... what do you want me to know?"

"I'm okay, brother. I have a different life in another otherworldly dimension, but I'm okay. I'm happy."

Hank sighed as a heavy wrecking ball of guilt began to float away from his shoulders, making him feel as light as a bird. "You're not dead? But I thought I killed you in that swing accident."

"That was never your fault. You must learn to accept that. It was an accident, nothing more. It ended my earthly existence, but gave me another more divine purpose outside of the mortal realm."

"So, there is life after death?"

"I'm living proof, if you'll pardon the expression."

Hank watched the wrecking ball float higher and higher until it disappeared into a cloud of white, powdery dust. Then, he said, "It's a miracle."

"That it is, my brother. But the Supreme Being works in mysterious ways. I'm here to save you. I'm here to assure you that I'm okay, it was never your fault, and from this day forward you have to get over the guilt, stop blaming yourself, and start living your life and begin living up to your true potential."

Hank was overcome with emotion. Tears of joy began streaming down his face. "Thank you, sis. I... I love you."

"I love you, too, dear brother," Lisa said. "Please, change for me, change for yourself, and change for the positive contribution you can still make to the world." Then Lisa rushed into her brother's open arms and embraced him in a tight hug. "Don't worry," she whispered into his ear. "I'll never leave you."

***

"Don't ever leave me, sis. Don't ever leave me."

The sound of his own voice startled Hank awake and he sat up in bed, looking left and right, right and left, frantically before it registered that he was indeed in his own bed, in his own bedroom, in his Vancouver apartment.

But everything was not the same. It was pretty far from the same. He jumped out of bed with the exuberance and enthusiasm of an overly rambunctious teen and began dancing around his bedroom singing, "My sister Lisa is alive... my sister is okay... my sister is happy... my sister is healthy... my sister loves me... and it's not my fault... oh, no, not my fault..."

He stopped suddenly, thinking for a split-second that perhaps he'd taken leave of his senses. But it was more than that. Something wasn't right. In his explosive bliss, he'd forgotten all about his aching back. Yet it wasn't aching anymore. He ran his hand down to the injured spot, feeling for the swollenness. It was as smooth as silk.

"Yippee," he shouted, jumping for joy and resuming a little dance number around his bedroom. "It's a miracle. Lisa cured me. The Supreme Being cured me."

"There's still hope for you," he said to his grinning reflection in the bathroom mirror a little later. Even his face looked fresher. Gone were the dark circles under his eyes. Even his deep blue eyes, identical to Lisa's, looked brighter and more alert.

As he reached for his shaver, he caught another glimpse of his reflection. Disbelieving, he moved closer to the mirror. Over his left eyebrow, he noticed a drop of blood. Sure enough, the three-inch scar resulting from the head injury he'd suffered from that fateful swing accident so many years ago had started to bleed.

He wiped it with a clean facecloth and examined it closer. It had been sliced almost surgically yet superficially. A much greater understanding of what had happened to him began to sink in and his body began to twitch with the epiphany.

He hadn't been dreaming at all. He'd dream-teleported, gone back in time, and then shot forward to another dimension where he'd been saved by Lisa. And now, here he was back in the so-called real world.

"It's a miracle, all right," he said to his refection. "It's a bloody miracle."

After showering, and then cleaning, disinfecting, and bandaging the small cut, which he was confident would heal in no time, he made a pot of coffee, finished one cup, and then decided a few calls were in order. He could barely contain the urge to start dancing around his apartment and singing his heart out again, but he wasn't sure his neighbors would appreciate it. And one part of him thought this was all a dream and he'd wake up, be in severe pain, and everything would be as miserable as it had been when he'd gone to bed last night.

He dialed Deborah and got her voice mail. "Hey, Deb, first of all, I wanna apologize if I offended you with my scrooge attitude about Christmas the other day. Merry Christmas to you, and I hope I get the chance to see you before the holidays."

He thought the Supreme Being would forgive a small white lie. "I bought you a Christmas present and I'd love to give it to you before Christmas. Bye for now. Take care."

Overflowing with excitement, Hank then got his sister Andrea on the phone.

"I didn't think I'd hear from you today, of all days," she said.

"What do you mean, sis?"

A long pause. Then she said, "You do realize that today is December 15th, the anniversary of our sister's death? You usually go into complete hibernation mode around this time."

In the fog of his earlier self-pity, depression, and self-loathing, it actually hadn't dawned on Hank. But it struck him now as the divine intervention of the Supreme Being, as Lisa had called Him. Or Her.

"I saw Lisa," Hank said. "I mean really saw her. She's okay."

"You saw her?" Andrea's voice cracked with emotion. "I wanna hear all about it."

"And I know the perfect time to tell you. Is that Christmas dinner invitation still open?"

"Of... of course. It's always open. You're my brother, and I love you."

"I love you, too." Hank felt his cheeks moisten with tears. "Please forgive me for being such an asshole yesterday."

"Forget about it. I know you hate Christmas."

"Not anymore, Andrea. I think from now on I'm gonna start loving it."

"Oh my God. This is a miracle."

"Merry Christmas, sis. Merry Christmas."

The End

Also by William Blackwell

Phantom Rage, Poison Rage, Infected Rage
Nightmare's Edge
Resurrection Point
Brainstorm
Rule 14
Assaulted Souls
Assaulted Souls II
Assaulted Souls III
Blood Curse
Black Dawn
The Strap
The End is Nigh
Orgon Conclusion
Freaky Franky
The Witch's Tombstone
The Dark Menace
Tales of Damnation
In Your Dreams
Macabre Alley
A Head for an Eye

In Your Dreams Preview

"On the surface, it's a gripping horror thriller with brutal, shocking twists. But beneath that, it's a thought-provoking exploration of obsession, loneliness, and the terrifying power our subconscious holds over us. The writing is bold, cinematic, and immersive—it reminded me of a cross between Clive Barker and early Stephen King, yet with a unique, modern edge." Amazon

Alienated from humanity, Oliver Gimble is a self-indulgent sloth who finds vicarious comfort in binge-watching horror movies and gorging on junk food. During sleep, he escapes into a meticulously constructed dream world where he discovers carnal delight with an enigmatic woman called Stella.

His bizarre lifestyle begins to unravel when he meets Carmen Weathersby, a lonely woman, who in Oliver's mind's eye mysteriously transforms into Stella, the woman of his dreams. But soon Oliver realizes Stella is actually interfering with his new relationship and will go to any lengths, even murder, to possess him.

When Carmen's elderly mother suffers a heart attack, fingers point to Stella.

Suddenly, people close to Carmen start dying—brutally and inexplicably.

Careening helplessly down into a cryptic and otherworldly realm somewhere between reality and perception, Carmen and Oliver struggle to try and solve the macabre mystery before it's too late.

A multi-layered, horrifying journey of self-discovery, *In Your Dreams* examines the powerful and shocking connections between our conscious and subconscious worlds—boldly questioning the very nature of reality.

About the Author

Canadian dark fiction author William Blackwell studied journalism at Mount Royal University and English literature at The University of British Columbia. He worked as a journalist and a newspaper editor for many years before pursuing his passion for storytelling. His novels have been characterized as graphic, edgy, and at times terrifying. Currently living on a secluded acreage on Prince Edward Island, Blackwell finds much of his inspiration from Mother Nature, odd people, traveling, and bizarre nightmares.

Author Comments

Thank you for reading this book. I would be eternally grateful if you would post a book review on your favorite book retailer website. A positive review is the highest compliment a writer can receive. Reviews are crucial to the success of any author and they help readers discover new books. You don't have to say much. A few sentences will suffice.

In other news, I have a gift for you. Complete the signup form below with your name and email address and download a FREE copy of *Resurrection Point*, a dark tale about the horrifying consequences of experimenting with death and resurrection. You're only agreeing to be kept up to date on blog posts, new releases, and freebies. I promise I won't spam you and you can unsubscribe at any time.

Thanks again for your support.

http://www.wblackwell.com/free-ebook/